William Taylor
Secret Lives

SCHOLASTIC

For my very good friend Ellen Gould

Scholastic Children's Books,
Scholastic Publications Ltd,
7-9 Pratt Street, London NW1 0AE, UK

Scholastic Inc.,
730 Broadway, New York, NY 10003, USA

Scholastic Canada Ltd,
123 Newkirk Road, Richmond Hill,
Ontario, Canada L4C 3G5

Ashton Scholastic Pty Ltd,
PO Box 579, Gosford, New South Wales,
Australia

Ashton Scholastic Ltd,
Private Bag 1, Penrose, Auckland,
New Zealand

First published by Ashton Scholastic Ltd, New Zealand, 1992

First published in the UK by Scholastic Publications Ltd, 1994

Text copyright © William Taylor 1992

ISBN 0 590 55474 3

Printed by Cox & Wyman Ltd, Reading, Berks

10 9 8 7 6 5 4 3 2 1

Chapter 1

"No thanks. That's fine." She shook her head and put her hand over her glass to prevent yet another refill. "No. No, not just now," as, regardless, a slug of the sweet and sticky orange liquid poured over her fingers.

"Oops! Sorry. Didn't go on your dress, did it?" said the girl doing the pouring.

"No. No, I'm fine. Really I am."

"It's good stuff," the pourer giggled. "I know what's in it."

"Mmm. Good," sounding doubtful. And then she smiled. "It's just I'm not a very quick drinker."

"Plenty more where that came from when you're ready. Drink up!" Almost an order, and the pourer moved off with her jug to more receptive glasses.

What was she doing here? Beth Paterson blinked and wiped a hand across her sweating forehead and then looked around. Why had she come? She hadn't wanted to. She folded her arms quite tightly about her, hunched slightly, and shivered although the late afternoon was warm, the sun was shining and the black clouds on the horizon were no more than a threat that would likely pass.

"What am I doing here?" Beth whispered this time. She shook her head again and wondered how soon she could leave without upsetting anyone. Grin and bear it. She shrugged slightly. Taking her own advice she pasted a passable smile on her face and tapped with her fingers to the rhythm of the music blaring from a stereo. Music that had been and gone a month, two months ago back home.

Home? This was home now. For the time being. For a year, anyway. For a year at least.

"Do you good to go to a party," her aunt had said. "You'll enjoy it once you get there. Most of them are nice kids and — and . . . well, you must get out and about."

"I don't want to go, Stella," Beth had said.

"You'll be in school with them, honey. Be a good idea to get to know one or two before school starts. They're nice kids," she repeated, "and it was nice of them to invite you." She did not add that it had taken more than a bit of phoning around to find out what was on, where it was on, who was giving it and how to wangle that invite.

"I've got nothing to wear, Stella. Besides, I don't know what they wear here for Saturday afternoon fooling around a pool. And I bet there's booze."

"Likely nothing stronger than Coke, honey," said her aunt. "Or maybe a little of that very light ale stuff. I think the Macaulays are Baptists or Buddhists or something and don't drink. And you've got a whole wardrobe — a whole bedroomful — of stuff to wear."

The Macaulays might well be Baptists or Buddhists but it sure wasn't stopping someone spiking just about everything liquid with a plentiful supply of vodka, Beth observed.

She might well have brought a bedroomful of stuff with her but it sure wasn't like the gear being worn around this pool. The clothes, like the music, were a step or two behind. Not much, but enough to be noticeable.

"Hi!"

"Hello."

"Can I sit down?"

"I don't know," said Beth, "can you?"

"Smart." He raised his eyebrows, smiled slightly and, pulling a chair towards her, sat. "I'm Vic. Who're you?"

"Beth Paterson," she moved her chair slightly further from him and edged over in the seat. She didn't smile.

He looked at her for a moment, clicked his fingers, and smiled again. "Gotcha!" he said.

"What d'you mean?" She did not want to talk to him.

"You're staying with old Stella — Miss Gordon, I mean. She's our art teacher and you're her—her—her little sister." Vic edged his chair closer again to Beth.

"Niece," said Beth. "I'm her niece."

"Yeah. That's it," said Vic. "Mum told me." He looked around him. "What d'you reckon?"

"What do you mean?" Beth asked.

"All this." He waved his hand, taking in the jumble of sunlit colour, the music, the noise. "Great, eh?"

"It's a good party," said Beth carefully. She went to edge away from him again but decided to sit her ground and stop playing musical chairs.

"Oh, yeah," said Vic. "You look bored out of your tree, if you ask me." A slight sneer. "Either that or we aren't good enough for you out here in the sticks."

"No," she protested, plastering the smile more firmly in place. "That's silly. It's a very good party. It's—it's just that I don't know anyone here."

"Yeah, well, you know me now," said Vic. "Reckon that's a big plus."

"Reckon that's a major worry," cut in the girl with the jug of drink as she filled Beth's glass, giving no chance for a refusal this time. "I see you've met Victor," she grinned at Beth, looking her up and down. "Still, I reckon you could handle him."

"Hey," said Victor, dragging out the sound. "Tell me about it! What have I done?" he kidded, smiling broadly and throwing up his hands in mock surrender.

"What haven't you done," said the girl. "Keep an eye on this one, Beth. He's lethal," — she looked at Vic — "or least he likes to think he is. Now, make yourself useful, Victor, and keep Beth's glass full. I'm sick of pouring drinks. I'm gonna have some fun."

"I really must be. . ." Beth began.

"That was our hostess. I suppose you know that," said Vic, one eye on the retreating back of the other girl and one eye on Beth. "That's Brenda."

"Yes, I do know," said Beth.

4

"And what was it you really must be doing?" he asked.

"Eh?"

"You were saying?"

"Oh—oh, yes. It's just that I really must be going soon," said Beth quickly. "Got a lot to do," she added.

"You don't have to go. Not yet. You only just got here," said Vic. "And I want to get to know you."

"Why?" asked Beth. "There's nothing much to know."

"Oh, I dunno," Vic looked Beth up and down and with a show of obvious appreciation of what he saw. "From where I'm sitting there's quite a lot. Why're you here?"

"Brenda invited me," Beth shrugged and looked around her. What on earth could she do to get away from this guy?

"I didn't mean that. Why've you come to Gray's Valley?"

Her reply was lost in the commotion of three of Brenda's guests being thrown into the pool and an attempted rescue by half of the remainder, the forcible dunking of a couple of the throwers and a barrage of beer and Coke cans into the water.

"Why've you come here?" Vic asked again, after the pool noise had dropped to roughly the same level as the hot, loud music.

Beth looked for escape. There was none. Her eyes darted as she scouted for a possible bolt-hole. Nothing. "I—er. . ."

"Yeah. Go on."

5

She had rehearsed it often enough, knowing the question would surely be asked. She was hesitant. "I—I wasn't getting on too good at home . . . School wasn't going as well as it should . . ." She turned to Vic and gave him a full, hard smile. "What's it they say — a change is as good as a rest?"

"Yeah — but Gray's Valley?" Vic groaned. "Hell, if I lived anywhere else, anywhere else at all, you couldn't get me here with a shotgun shoved —"

"It's not too bad," Beth broke in, looking down into the shrieking turbulence of the pool in which half of Brenda's guests were now drowning the other half and washing the poolside furniture at the same time.

"It's the pits," said Vic miserably. "Look at them all," he followed her stare into the pool. "This is the highlight of their summer for most of 'em. Brenda's party. Geez, she's been having these parties since we were all about eleven. Five or six years of Brenda's parties. Geez! Same crowd, same place. Almost the same games except when we were eleven we called it Sardines and now we call it something else and it starts much later, but it's sure the same thing. And now she gets her old lady and her old man to go away for the weekend and not just out for the night." He looked at her. "Let's go," he said.

"What d'you mean?" asked Beth, startled.

He looked at her, not smiling. "Let's go. Leave. Let's split. I've got my car. You wanna go home? I'll take you home."

"No. Er — no." Trapped. "Um, my aunt, Stella, she's calling for me." Surely not this.

"We'll phone her," said Vic. "You can phone her. Gray's Valley's got phones you know."

More trapped. "Well ... um ... maybe I just might stay a bit longer." Beth's face worked and her mouth dried. "Yeah. I won't go just yet. And it'd be rude," she added, unconvincingly.

"You were going to go ten minutes ago. Would've been ruder then," said Vic quietly. "Look, I'll drive you round the town — spot the sights." He snorted. "What there are of them. Then I'll take you back out to your aunt's. Not a problem. Let me show you beautiful Gray's Valley," he smiled.

Beth looked at him, the slight smile on his clear and open face. He smoothed his longish fair hair with one hand as he gestured for her to come with him with the other. She gulped. "Okay. I—I have got a bit of a headache. I'll just say thanks to Brenda." She kept her eyes on him. He looked safe enough.

"No need," said Vic, quickly. "I'll tell her." He moved to the poolside where Brenda seemed to be conducting an underwater wrestling match.

Beth caught the look of surprise that crossed the other girl's face as Vic bent down to whisper in her ear. She noticed the quick glance that Brenda shot between Vic and herself. Brenda moved to stand but Vic kept a hand on her shoulder and laughed a quick farewell.

By now Beth had moved from the pool. She missed seeing the nudge of Vic's knee that sent Brenda, squealing, to join her guests in the pool.

"C'mon," he said quickly to Beth. "Let's go.

Brenda says she's sorry about your headache and come back later if you feel like it and the fun never starts till well after dark. Fun? Huh! C'mon."

"Look, I don't mind ringing Stella and she won't mind coming to get me. I don't want . . ."

"C'mon."

The glare of the late afternoon sun on the water of the pool, combined with the heat, had given Beth a headache and she was sweating. She gave in and Vic led her to his car. The fresher air out on the street, while still hot, revived her slightly. As he held open the car door for her, Beth swallowed nervously and told herself not to be stupid. This was nothing. Nothing at all. Just a quite nice, quite pleasant, quite quiet guy giving her a ride home. What was there to worry about? Been through it a hundred — well, a couple of dozen — times before. What could happen? Broad daylight, too, and Stella's just a ten-, fifteen-minute drive. It was all okay. Everything was okay.

"Thanks," she said, as he helped her in.

"Yeah. We got good manners round here." He grinned, pulled a monkey-face at her through the front windscreen and got into the driver's seat.

"This yours?" she asked.

"What?"

"The car."

"My car? Yep. Sure is."

"Lucky."

"I worked for it. I worked for it since I was ten. Saved every cent," Vic patted the dashboard. "She's my baby. You like it?"

8

"It's good."

"She's not new." Seriously.

"No."

"But she'll do." Vic started the motor. It idled, purring. "Wanted a motorbike but my old man wouldn't let me. I'm glad, now. Wasn't too glad back then, but I am now."

"Why?" Beth asked.

"You can do a lot more things with a car than you can with any stuffing motorbike. You smoke?" He took out a pack of cigarettes and offered it to her.

"God, no," said Beth.

Vic shrugged. "Live long enough in Gray's and you soon will. They all do," he gestured with a thumb back towards the house. "Nothing much else to do round here. You do dope?" He rolled down the window.

"No," said Beth. "No, I don't," and she looked at him.

"That's cool," said Vic. "Neither do I."

"Can we go now?" Beth moistened her lips and wished she had the guts to get out of the car. "You know where I live?"

"Sure. No hurry." He gunned the motor, put it into gear, reversed, changed gear again and slipped the car easily from the haphazard crush of other vehicles. "Remember? We're gonna spot a few sights."

"I'd rather go straight home," said Beth.

Vic ignored her.

Clouds rolled in; black, looming. Ate up the sun. Thunder threatened. The heat did not lessen.

With a half-smile on his face, Vic eyed Beth but

said nothing. He slid a cassette into the dashboard stereo, and turned up the volume on the beat of heavy, raw metal. "Driving music," he grinned. "Right?" and he geared up his smile and his car. "We've seen the town now," he said, nodding at the windscreen. "We're gonna drive into that storm." He headed out of the village and onto the highway. "We'll hit that little sucker head-on. Let's drive!"

Beth shuddered, said nothing. There was nothing to say. She sank back as much as the bucket seat allowed and knew she had made a wrong choice.

Chapter 2

"I'm going out for a pig," Bruno Petrie called through the open doorway behind him.

"What d'you say? What? What was that?"

"I'm going out to look for a pig," he called louder. "Couple of hours, no more."

"Can't hear you. Speak up, boy!"

Bruno sighed, shook his head and turned back into the house. He walked across to the cassette player and lowered the volume. "If you didn't blast the socks off every living thing with old Maria Callas twenty-four hours a day, you'd hear what I said," he muttered.

"Nothing wrong with my hearing, boy. Turn her back up again. I'm missing the best part, the part where she—"

"You know it off by heart, Arch. I know I sure do. Hum it in your head." Bruno looked across to his father. "I'm going out for a pig," he said again.

"Why?"

Bruno smiled. "First, because I'm sick of listening to Maria Callas and I can't hear myself think. Second, if I don't go now it's going to bucket down later on and I'll never spot the sign. And third, because Les and Ray want one. They've got a load of Germans due in to fish the lower reaches and no wild pork in the freezer and they go for wild pig in a big way."

"Turn her up again — no," the old man changed his mind. "Wind it back first and then turn her up. How long'll you be?"

"I said a couple of hours."

"Don't know why you can't leave the poor dumb creatures alone." It was the old man's turn to mutter. "It's going to rain."

Bruno sighed again. "I know, Arch. I already said that." He fiddled with the rewind control on the machine. "You got everything you want?"

"Don't ask stupid questions, boy. Of course I haven't got everything I want. Must be obvious even to you. Now then, turn her on and get out."

"Cup of tea first?"

"Not the way you make it," said his father.

"Bad mood today, eh Arch?" said Bruno.

"Go on. Get out. And I hope you don't find a pig."

"Small chance of that," said Bruno. "They're everywhere at the moment. But I'll just make you a cuppa first, whether you want one or not," he grinned.

"Black. One sugar. Shot of whisky," said his father.

"Sure, Arch," said Bruno, whistling along with a few bars of a mad scene with Callas. Reflecting on where the best place would be to look for a pig, and where he'd be less likely to get stuck in the mud on his old farm-bike when it came on to rain, Bruno made tea for his father.

He was still whistling to Callas as he tightened his belt, shouldered his rifle, stowed a minimum of wet weather gear into a saddle-bag and called up Primrose — pig-dog and pet — and mounted his bike. The motorbike sputtered into half life and puttered down the steep hill leading away from the house, well in the wake of Primrose the dog.

Bruno took in the sight of the gathering storm rising from the horizon and decided to hunt as near to the house as possible. No sense ending up half drowned and mud bound for the sake of any pig even if the cash his catch would earn would be more than welcome. With school starting again in a couple of days he needed every dollar he could lay his hands on. Every dollar and then some.

The perils of riding the ill-formed, overgrown track down into the gullies and scrub of his father's property soon took his mind off opera and he stopped whistling, listening instead for any indication that his dog, well ahead by now, had got onto the scent of something. No sound. It didn't worry him. Primrose and Bruno were a pair, a couple, indivisible when it came to chasing pigs, each knowing the thinking, the working of the other. If need be, one call — two at the outside — and his dog would be back with him.

The old bike clunked and lurched to the bottom of the hill and there Bruno stopped. He glanced up at the sky and clouds, looked at his watch and shrugged. He parked the bike and his rifle, half stripped off and flung himself into a growth of soft, green fern, stretching out to enjoy the heat of the sun on his exposed skin. Primrose could do the work.

Primrose did work. Bruno, idle, day-dreamed,

puzzling yet again as to how on earth he could get his hands on at least a moderate dollop of dollars, enough to see him and Arch through the year. Enough to, just maybe, get him a half decent motorbike, or even an old truck. They would manage, he knew that. After all, they always had, but these days it sure was hard. Harder now that he had school to worry about as well, and as sure as wild pigs were wild pigs he wasn't giving up on that. Not now.

Ray and Les at the Lodge? Not really an option. They were just about as broke as him and Arch, and had a mortgage bigger than Mt Gray. Sure they paid him — as well as they were able — for the gardening, the pigs, and for the other odds and ends of game he supplied for their guests, but Bruno knew they weren't finding it easy.

Besides, it just wasn't that simple. School took just about every working hour, every waking hour that God gave. It wasn't a matter of just catching up on all the years he had missed. If only that was all it was! After all, he had had to start right back from scratch, almost as if he had never been to school at all. Just one more year. One more year and he'd be finished. One more year and he'd be twenty! Then what?

Money. School. School. Money. And Arch. What in God's good name was to happen to Arch?

Bruno Petrie raised himself on his elbow, looked again at the sky, looked again at his watch and called his dog. Once. Twice. Then waited. As if by magic, in less than three minutes the animal was back at his side. "Useless dog! Where're them pigs, eh?" He fondled Primrose's ears. "And don't you dare lie down, useless dog. We're off. Should be time to make it over to the old quarry before you, me'n the bike get drowned," he muttered. "Shot a couple of goats up there one, two weeks back. If that hasn't drawn a pig or two nothing will. Come on you lazy devil," he patted the dog's rump and heaved himself to his feet. "Come on you lazy devil," he said to himself again, chuckled, then sat back down. "Okay. You can take five, dog. Me, too."

Bruno and his dog took twenty. By the time he had persuaded his bike that it still had its half life and they had headed up and out of the gully, the black clouds of the horizon were choking the sun and the heat grew more intense, more oppressive and the first faint rumble of thunder echoed in the little valleys and gullies of his land.

Chapter 3

Ten minutes. Twenty minutes. Vic drove fast, flat out. The storm clawed everything into itself and it was black. Not even the near full volume of the car stereo could drown the wild reverberations of the enveloping thunder nor the lashing beat of the rain.

Vic's eyes glistened and his lips were drawn back in a half grin that was no smile at all. His speed did not lessen and the rain pelted, powered horizontal, in an incessant, almost saucer-sized, pelleting against the windscreen. The wipers lost the battle; a useless flap-flapping that did little to clear the vision from the vehicle.

At first Beth flinched at the fury of it all. Then she gave up, glazed her eyes, and slumped back in her seat. She said nothing to Vic, knowing that at this moment he was hardly aware of her existence. The speed, the danger — they were not what at heart disturbed her. Another time, another place, another driver, and the excitement and thrill might have done for her what it seemed to be doing for him. Not now. All she wanted was to be home, back at Stella's. Home? Yes, it was home.

Beth hugged her arms close around her and

retreated into herself, half wondering where the road might lead, how long he would drive and how she would manage to get herself out of the situation.

As suddenly as it had engulfed them, the storm freed them. Not back into the sunlight but into a thin, warm, misty grey drizzle. The evening was darkening. With a slither and a wrenching slide Vic pulled the car over, at almost full speed, into a small highway rest area. They stopped.

"Whew!" he shook his head. "That sure was something else."

"Where are we?" Beth asked dully.

"Halfway up the old saddle road," he pointed out the window into the mist. "We come up from down there." He leaned back. "That sure was good. Bloody good. Done that as quick as if it was fine." He lit a cigarette.

"We better be getting back," said Beth.

"Why?" He sounded surprised. "Thought we'd cruise on over the saddle. There's a burger joint — sort of diner — just over the other side. Grab us a burger and drive on."

"I've got to get home," she said. "Stella."

"Stuff Stella. You're not a baby," he sneered. "You're not her kid."

"I want to go home," said Beth.

"Later," Vic ferreted through a container of cassette tapes. "Check these out. Put on something you like. Anything. Some good stuff there."

She made no move to do as he asked. "I want to go home," she repeated.

"Later." He picked out a tape, ejected the heavy metal and shot the new one home. It was much the same as the one it replaced. "Later," he repeated. "Let's get us a burger," and they were off again, up and winding into the gloom of the forested hills. Victor rummaged in the driver's side glovebox and dragged out a bottle. "Yeah. Yeah. Thought I still had something left in this little mother. Here." He unscrewed the cap and held it out to her.

"No," she shook her head. "No." More definitely.

"Please yourself." He shrugged and then drank from the bottle. "Good stuff. Sure you won't?"

"I don't drink."

"You did at Brenda's party," he reminded her.

"It was fruit juice."

"Like hell it was fruit juice," Vic said.

She sighed. "Well, all right then. I guess she had a bit of something in it, but not much. Anyway, I don't drink."

Vic turned down the stereo and half turned in his seat to face her. "Why are you here? Why've you come here to Gray's Valley?"

"I told you."

"Yeah. And that's not what I heard. I heard things. Go on. You can tell me. You can trust me."

Suddenly she was angry. "It's none of your damn business," she yelled at him and turned the stereo volume further down. "It's none of your business at all."

"That's better," said Vic, taking a corner too wide.

"And what d'you mean I can trust you? Like hell

I can trust you. You were going to take me home . . ."

"Still am," he grinned. "Like later." His smile broadened and he turned away from her, murmuring, repeating, "Like later."

They stopped at the diner. While Vic went in to buy food Beth toyed with the idea of getting out of the car and walking off. But where to? She had only a vague idea of where she was. She could phone her aunt. Surely there'd be a phone up here. Yes. Yes. That's what she would do. She got out of the car just as Vic was returning.

"Where you going?"

"The ladies. The loo," she said.

"It's the other way," he pointed.

"I want some gum," she said, and walked into the diner.

"Sorry, dear. Line's down. Always happens these summer storms. It'll be down and out for days. Nothing too urgent, dear? Sure?"

"No. It's fine," said Beth. "Thanks, anyway," and she returned to the car. "I don't want one," she said to Vic as he offered her a greasy, brown-paper bag. "I told you I didn't want one."

"Please yourself," he said. "I'll eat it. They're good. Plenty of onion. Sure like onion in a burger." He started the car.

"Are we going back now?" she asked.

He revved the engine as he ate. "Nah."

Beth tried to reason with him. "Look, Vic, I'm tired. I'm very tired and I do want to go home. Really I do. Look, I haven't been too well and I'm not feeling

19

all that good . . ." and then a hint of promise. "Look, Vic . . . maybe some other time . . ." She was angry. Not scared of him, but angry. She fought not to let the anger show, sensing that if she did it would only goad him to further excess.

Suddenly he appeared to give in. "Okay," he said. "That's cool. Yeah. Stink night, anyway. We'll go back to Brenda's?"

"No," said Beth. "Well, you can go where you like but I want to go home."

"Okay," said Vic as he drove from the parking lot and headed back up into the darkening, misted hills. He did not drive fast. Just a deliberate, moderate speed and he said nothing, turning up the volume of the car stereo.

Beth sat, tense at first as if not believing him. Soon, however, the steady momentum of the car and an absence of further persistence from its driver lulled her part way into a sense of security. She leaned back in her seat, her eyes half closed. She did not notice until too late that they had left the highway. It was his muttered, "Come on, Vic. Hang a left, hang a left, mate," that brought her to.

Suddenly she was fully alert, alarmed. "What's this?" she snapped. "Where are we? This isn't the main road."

"Nah," he grinned. "Sure isn't."

"Where are we going?"

"Relax. Just up the old quarry. Relax, it's a good road. Well," — they jolted heavily — "bits of it is. Told you we'd spot the sights," he laughed. "This sure is one famous local sight."

"Take — me — home," she said clearly, loudly.

"Always rabbits and things on the road up here at night. We'll do a few, eh?" He changed down gear as the road narrowed and the climb steepened. "Reckon we'll get us a bunny or six." He sped up and the headlights of the car picked up a startled and scurrying form. Vic tracked his prey with grim intensity, wheeling erratically onto the grassed verge, then back out onto the loose metal of the road in pursuit of the animal. "Gotcha!" he yelled. A slight bump. He did not stop.

Beth clung to her seat and said nothing.

The road widened and suddenly they bumped a descent through bracken, scrub and moonscape rock into a roughly formed amphitheatre. Vic stopped; stilled the engine. "The old quarry," he announced. "Quite a place, eh? See all them bunnies? We'll get 'em on the way back." He doused the car lights.

"I don't want to be here," said Beth firmly. "You know I don't. Now, let's get out of here and you take me home."

"You don't want to go home," said Vic. "I know what you want and I bet you done it a hundred times before. Come here." He grabbed at her arm, roughly forcing her to face him. With his free hand he took her other arm, brutally and with enough speed and force to jerk her head back.

Beth was not surprised, nor even frightened. She had known all along that this would be the probable course of events and it was now over to her to do what she could to sabotage the outcome he expected. "Jerk!" she half hissed, pulling away from him. The fingernails of one hand raked at his cheek and his reaction was enough to allow her to free her other arm. She groped for the handle of the car door.

"No you don't, bitch!" he yelled, as he reached across and got his hand to the handle before she had a chance. With a quick flick it came away in his hand. She was trapped. "What you gonna do now?" he jeered. "What you gonna do now?"

She said nothing, desperately trying to hold him at bay in the rapidly increasing heat of the car cab. She was tight-lipped, and breathing hard.

"I know what you want," he lunged again at her. "I sure know what you want," and he moved his body half across hers, pinning her to the passenger door.

The stench of his boozy onion breath in the hot enclosed space made her gag. "Get off me, you — you . . ."

"Shut up!" he yelled into her face and began pulling at her clothing. "And don't bother trying that window," as she almost managed to get a hand to the window winder. "Only goes down an inch. You're not goin' nowhere." He grabbed more furiously at the thin knit top she was wearing. The fabric stretched and gave but did not tear. He now had both of her wrists in his grip, one forced back against the window and the other against the car seat; a very strong grip.

Through her gritted teeth she spat at him, "You little runt. Don't think you're gonna get me like this, you . . ." and she took him absolutely, fully by surprise:

she dropped her head and sank her teeth into his wrist. Beth tasted blood.

Victor squealed and jerked back, clutching at his injury. Beth made the most of what she knew would be only seconds of freedom. Leaning slightly towards him, she raised a clenched fist as far as she was able and brought it down with full force right between his legs. Vic screamed, and grabbed his crotch. The force of her movement had dragged Beth across the front seat and almost half on top of Vic. Her free hand grabbed at the steering wheel for support but landed first on the car horn. It sounded loud. As she tried to right herself, Beth's hand slipped from the horn and onto the windscreen wiper and headlight controls, activating both.

Directly ahead, in the full and sudden blaze of light from the car was a motorbike. Motionless. Equally still, and astride the machine — booted, jeaned and jacketed and wearing a black balaclava — was its rider. Draped half across the handlebars of the bike was one very dead wild pig.

Beth screamed.

Chapter 4

The full fury of the storm had caught Bruno, Primrose and the motorbike as they headed from one pigless gully into its neighbour. Dog and owner took what little shelter was offered by an ancient, half-dead macrocarpa tree. Bruno pulled an old pair of jeans on over his shorts, buttoned himself into a not-quite-waterproof jacket and worked his head into the only hat he had; an old balaclava. Then he sat down to wait out the worst of the deluge, water trickling down the back of his neck. "Hell, dog! It's all your fault. You're gettin' past it," he complained, as Primrose snuggled closer against him for maximum protection. "We'll never get us a pig now."

The dog whimpered as a particularly vicious clap of thunder boomed above them.

"It'll have to be the old quarry and back down the road now. God help us if there's a cop on the highway. No helmet. No lights, even." He grinned. "No pig, neither," and he giggled. "It's all your fault, dog. You said I could sleep." He patted the animal. Primrose poked her head onto Bruno's outstretched leg and whimpered some more. Bruno softly stroked between the animal's ears and down its muzzle. "It's okay, pig-dog," he chuckled softly. "Well, no-pig pig-dog. Should shoot you, eh? That's what happens to dogs that don't earn their keep. Can't afford to keep a no-pig pig-dog. No way. Can't afford to keep me, even. Big-time no-pig pig-hunter. What d'you say to that?"

As the rain eased to a drizzle, the gullies steamed with a warm mist that quickly enshrouded them in a soft, grey, dusky gloom. It worried neither man nor dog. Both knew this land well.

Bruno sighed, got to his feet and prayed hard that his bike would start. It would not be the first time he'd had to push, pull and manoeuvre the dead machine back up these hills, and in similar slithery conditions. However, this time it sprang into fitful existence at first kick. Astride the bike, he used his legs to help propel it along a series of narrow goat tracks back up into the hills, fording what would have been just damp spots earlier in the afternoon but were now instant rivers. He knew every track and how to use it. Where to slide, where to slither. He'd done it many times before.

He silently cursed the terrain. Primrose had gone. Near the crest of the first hill the unexpected happened. To his right and in a thicket of scrub the loud and excited bark of his dog told him she had found something.

Bruno stilled the bike's engine, propped it against a bank and listened. The bark persisted. She had something bailed, all right. Unslinging his rifle, Bruno checked his belt for his knife and headed through the gloom towards the yelping dog, sending up a prayer that if it were a pig it would stay exactly and precisely where it now stood. If it ran, he was not going after it. Not in this light.

Bruno's prayer was answered. Even before he reached the site of the barking a high-pitched squeal told him his dog had pinned the prey.

It wasn't a big pig. A small sow, not much bigger than the dog that had caught it. Big enough though. Swiftly, expertly, Bruno dispatched the animal, bled and gutted it, heaved it across his shoulder and headed from the scrub back to his bike. "Not too bad, dog," he grinned. "Not too dusty."

Again the bike started but the added burden of the pork made the going slower. Bruno stopped on the ridge of the rise leading down into the old quarry, shivered slightly against a first wafting of cooler night air rising from the small basin, and pulled down the balaclava. He didn't notice the parked car at the foot of the rise.

Progress was easier now, the quarry tracks much better than the farm valleys. The prospect of being no more than a fifteen, twenty minute ride from home sped him faster. He was almost upon the car when a faint flicker of moonlight from a clearing but still cloud-scudded sky caught at the chrome of its front bumper.

It all happened at once. As the car headlights powered onto him and the horn sounded, Bruno jerked his machine to a shuddered and stalled halt. "What—what the hell . . ." he was yelling as he registered first the sound of the car horn and then the screaming. Not thinking for an instant that it may have been the sight of his own rather sinister appearance that was causing the commotion, Bruno was off the bike in an instant, letting it fall, pig and all, as he made for the car. "What the hell . . .?" as he came to the driver's side.

Beth's mind groped its way through two terrors and decided, for no sound reason, that the more recent might be the lesser evil. "Get me out of here," she called.

Victor, shocked, frightened now, groaned. "She— she . . ."

Bruno summed up the situation in seconds. "Get out then!" he yelled at her as he leaned against the driver's side door.

"I can't," she yelled back. "He's got the bloody door handle and the window doesn't open!"

"Give her the handle, mate," said Bruno, threateningly.

Vic, terrified, felt around on the floor of the car, found the handle and passed it to Beth. She slipped it onto its shaft, got out, and stood shivering against the front mudguard. Vic tried to follow her in an effectual and painful dive across the gear lever. "No you don't, mate," said Bruno, very quietly, one hand on Vic's neck. "You okay? What happened?" he asked Beth.

"He—he . . ." She gulped, now almost as frightened of this new arrival as she had been of Vic.

"Try it on, eh, punk?" Bruno opened the door of

the car, pulled Vic from it and smacked him once, quite hard, before pushing him back into the driver's seat. He pulled Vic's head through the open window with one hand and rolled up the window with the other. Before slamming and locking the door, he took the keys from the ignition. "You okay?" he called to Beth again.

"Er . . ." said Beth. The sheer, brutal speed with which her rescuer had worked had stunned her.

Vic made a series of trapped sounds and waggled his hands about, trying to connect with door handle or window winder.

Bruno whistled up his dog and ordered the animal to a spot just beneath Vic's head. "Stay!" he commanded. "Don't try and get out, rat," he snarled at Vic. "Dog's worser'n me with dirt like you," he lied. "Stay!"

"What—what . . .?" said Vic, and then, "Don't—don't . . ."

Bruno's teeth showed very white in the mouth-hole of his black balaclava. "You just have a rest now," he said to Vic. "Looks like you could do with one. I'll be back to get you, and me dog," — he nodded at Primrose — "soon as I get her home." He pointed to Beth.

Beth found her voice. "Just—just show me the way out of here and I think I know how — how . . ." She shook her head and then felt the warmth of tears on her face. "Dammit!" she said softly and gritted her teeth. She wasn't going to cry in front of this grotesque thing, and most definitely not in front of the trapped and gurgling Vic. "Main road," she said. "Just show me the way to the main road."

"You're miles from home," said Bruno. "I'll take you," he grinned again, looking more evil than ever. "Nothing to worry about on my motorbike," he laughed, adding "if it even goes — and if it doesn't we'll both have to walk. We got no lights and no helmets but don't you worry. I know where Miss Gordon lives." He turned back to Vic. "You can look after my pig, pig," he said, and hoisted the bloodied carcass onto the bonnet of the car. "You look after it real good and I might let you go when I get back. Stay!" he again ordered Primrose.

"No, no, no, no, no . . ." gurgled Vic.

"Get on," he yelled to Beth over the spit and sputter of his bike motor. "You'll be okay. Know all these tracks real well. Had any sense, I reckon I'd take his car but I think you seen enough of the insides of that. Sure you're okay?"

"Yes, I'm okay," she yelled. "I wasn't far off okay when you turned up. I'd just thumped him one where it really hurt." Beth got on the bike behind Bruno.

Another balaclava grin. "Sure hasn't been old Vic's night, eh?"

"I just didn't know what I was going to do next," she said.

"I'll lend you my knife next time," said Bruno. "Just let me know."

All Beth said when he dropped her off at her aunt's house was, "Thanks a lot," as she ran up the path and into the house.

All her aunt said was, "You're home early, honey. Have a nice time?" and, "Pop the kettle on, hon."

Chapter 5

She looked at herself in the mirror. Went on looking. She pursed her lips and stared into her own eyes.

"Hurry up, honey," called her aunt. "There's a limit to how late I can be — and you've had no breakfast."

"Don't want any," Beth called back. "Just coffee'll do me."

"You can't just have coffee, for God's sake . . . What am I saying? You're not my kid and if all you want is coffee, have coffee. Just get a move on."

Beth grimaced into the mirror, pulled back her long, ash-blond hair and slipped a band around the whole hank at the nape of her neck. She winked at her own reflection, half smiling, "One day at a time, girl," she said softly. "One day at a time and today might be better than yesterday." She sighed. "And I don't know whether yesterday was better than the day before." She sighed again and the half-grin vanished. The expressionless face gazing back at itself was, she knew, unremarkable. Only the thick head of smokey-blond hair and the wide, big grey eyes saved her from downright plainness. The mouth too wide, the nose too big, the face too thin. Passable but unremarkable. The figure, athletic, broad-shouldered, not too bad.

None of which, neither the whole nor any of the individual components, had ever worried her.

She came out of her room and sat down with her aunt. "Finding it hard living with someone else, eh Aunty Stella?" Beth smiled at the older woman.

"Don't you Aunty Stella me, you little madam," Stella Gordon laughed. "And go on smiling a bit more. Haven't seen too much of that grin since you arrived. And, no, I'm not finding it hard having you here. Most of the time I don't even know you *are* here, more's the pity. Now, hurry up," — she flung her arms in a dramatic swing — "No! Don't bother. Why, why, why break the habit of a lifetime? I'm sure I'll be late for my own funeral. I'll make us both some toast."

"You don't mind me being here, Stella?" Beth asked quietly.

The woman looked at her niece. She spoke slowly and at the same time fumbled bread into the toaster. "I neither mind nor don't mind, honey." She paused. "I—I just hope it helps . . . just wish you'd—you'd talk about it." She paused again. "You're just so sort of closed up . . . sort of shut in, contained. I've said so many times — probably too many times — for you to talk about it to me." She smiled. "Don't you worry about how welcome you are. Do me a power of good to share things for a while. I'm getting far too set in my middle-aged ways."

Beth looked up at her aunt. "Sometime I might talk," she said. Her mouth twisted. "I might, Stella," and then she looked away.

"And now we really must hurry," said Stella. "Hell's bells! It's the first day of the term — of the year!" She tossed the toasted bread onto the table. "Gobble! Come on. Gobble, gobble, gobble!"

"Stella, who's a guy lives round here, rides an old motorbike and wears a balaclava?"

"Goodness, honey. Sounds absolutely ghastly. No idea. Some local hood or hoon. But you know me," she pointed to the jumble of paint pots, easels, and canvasses that spread like some vivid growth through virtually her whole cottage, "lose myself in this junk and I couldn't even tell you the time of day . . . and that reminds me . . ."

There was some advantage, Beth reflected, in starting a new school just for your last senior year. Fewer kids, less skylark hassle, and if you weren't one of the crowd, the in-crowd, it didn't really matter all that much. Certainly, for her, an easier entry than for most. Her aunt had taught for years at Gray's Valley High; she was a popular, much-loved eccentric whose chronic lateness bothered no one but herself. On one famous occasion, which had become well-embroidered in the telling, Stella Gordon had marched out onto the hall stage in the middle of a full, formal assembly wearing her oldest painter's smock, lugging several tins of paint and a box of brushes and singing at the top of her voice. Stopping dead in her tracks, and in mid note, she took one startled look at the assembled throng and said, "Good God, hons! I thought it was Sunday and I'm here to paint the backdrop for the show. Am I late or am I early? Tell me if I missed something." The whole place, staff and students, had exploded.

The dozen or so students in Beth's seventh form year had their own small cubby-hole common room, furnished with the battered cast-offs of many Gray's Valley homes. It was a place to gather, have a cup of coffee and exchange gossip. On her third day at the school Beth used the room for the first time in a vain attempt to find a spot of peace and quiet in which to unravel a timetable that had her in four places at once.

"Ah great! It's you. I wanted to have a chat with you but you sure know how to hide yourself away. I'll make us some coffee." It was Brenda Macaulay, party-giver. She looked at the papers Beth was thumbing through. "Heavens above, you're not worried about your timetable, are you?"

"Well . . ."

"They've never ever been known to get 'em right first shot. Not ever. Look, take my advice — if they've stuffed it up, and they always have, just don't turn up. Make the most of it. They won't know for yonks. My older brother, Mike, like he got five months into the year and no one noticed he'd never turned up for biology." Brenda poured half-boiled water into two mugs. "Anyway, put it away now. Get your aunt to sort it out for you at home." She shook her head and giggled. "No. You'd better not. God knows where you'd end up! Anyway, sorry you never got back to the party the other night . . ." A sly look.

"It was a good party," said Beth. "It was just . . ."

"*And* . . ." Brenda emphasised the word, "what on

earth did you do to poor Vic? Or, more to the point, what did he try to do to you? Tell me . . . you've gotta tell me."

"There's nothing to tell," said Beth. "He took me, well . . . well, he took me part way home."

"Ho, ho, ho," said Brenda. "No he didn't. Have you seen him? He only started back today. He's got one puffy eye that looks as if it was black, all these scratches on his face and it looks like he was half-strangled round his neck." She chuckled some more. "Lovely. Little el creepo, him. I was going to warn you, I really was, but he knocked me in the pool. Wow, you've sure got great hair. Just wish I could grow mine long. What'd he try?" Brenda patted her very short crop of blond-streaked, highlighted brown hair.

The friendliness of the other girl disarmed Beth. "You know exactly what he tried," she said, managing a small smile.

"Well, kid, you've sure done better than most of us, and I can't think of anyone round here he hasn't tried it on with. El creepo he may be, still, he's not all bad — if you don't let him get to the car door handle first, and it doesn't look like you let him get anywhere at all, much less first."

Their chat was cut short. Two other girls came in, fell on Brenda and loudly relived Saturday's party. Close on their heels came Victor Witt. He caught sight of Beth, but too late.

"Hey! Vic, Vic, Vicky," squealed Brenda. "I think you've met Beth Paterson. She's new here. You have met? Haven't you? Haven't you?" she drawled.

Shrieks of laughter from her mates. Beth started to gather her things together.

"Hey, Vic? What's up with your face?" called one of the others. "Had a tooth out, eh? Tooth fairy have to hold you down this time?"

Vic reddened, gave a half-sneer, half-snigger, shot a look of venom at Beth, turned on his heel and took off out the door.

"Tooth fairy try to strangle you, Vicky?" the other girl shrilled after him, and then the three of them got to work on Beth and it was some minutes before she could reasonably escape from the stuffy little room.

At nights she walked. Just on dusk, generally. Alone, as private as she needed to be.

I'll ask Brenda, she said to herself. I'll ask her if she knows who the man is with the balaclava and the motorbike. Then she pushed the thought aside. Who cared?

She would walk for an hour, often more. Usually there were no thoughts, no thinking, and she would walk slightly stooped, head down, arms folded across her stomach against the feeling of emptiness there that was not a nothingness but rather a real, full and aching pain.

When the thoughts did flood in she would talk to herself. Conversations between herself and her mother. Harsh, bitter talks. And the other conversations, painful in their pointlessness — and then she'd try not to talk but to walk harder, faster, further until there was nothing again, because talk was bad and didn't help. If talk went on there'd be tears. Tears in gusty, wrenching floods and she'd fall onto the grass or into the fern or scrub and have to howl it out until she was empty and there was nothing left except that hollow ache in her gut. She could put up with that.

Then she would go back to Stella's and her aunt would just smile and say nothing more than, "Put the kettle on, hon."

"Your inside, Stella, must be more tanned than a bit of leather," Beth would say, or something like that, forcing a smile.

There would be ten, fifteen minutes of banter, of saying nothing in particular, before one or the other would take off to bed.

Chapter 6

"Take this," said Lesley, handing Bruno a cheque.
"Look, man, we're sorry it can't be more but you
know the score, how things are."

"You don't need to give me this, Les." Bruno looked
at the two women and wished with all his heart that
he could afford to refuse their money.

"We're doing all right," said Ray. "The old cash
flow sure isn't everything it could be, but that" —
she nodded at the cheque — "is the least we can do
for someone we love who works for us for next to
nothing." She turned away and bent to pull a stray
weed from among the dahlias in the Lodge garden.

"Come on in," said Lesley. "The other least we can
do is have a drink to your having a great year. By the
way, the Germans loved the pork. Two of them are
back next week and want the kid goat in red wine thing
that Ray does. Any chance?"

Bruno smiled at the two of them. "If I've got to
chase goats all day, you'll have it. What was that about
a drink?"

They walked into the building, the place that for
years had been the dream of the two women and that,
in reality, had proved everything they had hoped for
. . . other than making their fortunes. Low-pitched,

shingled roofs with walls of natural river stone stood above a cedar base. Elegant, and fitting of the site, it nestled into a river bend surrounded by massed groves of silver birch and banks of native shrubs and ferns. Most of the shrubbery Bruno had uplifted from the scrub of his own land and shouldered across the ford to the Lodge site for replanting.

The women, Lesley Parker and Ray Sullivan, fiftyish both, were lifelong friends who had thrown aside the security of well-paid jobs and sunk everything they could lay their hands on into their dream of creating a fishing lodge on the banks of the river both had fished for a score of years. The lodge's six bedrooms slept twelve guests in some comfort and their food was fast becoming a byword. While they'd never make a fortune, they both knew they were lucky to be doing precisely what they wanted to do.

Apart from themselves, the rest of their staff was Bruno Petrie. Odd-job and handyman, gardener, dishwasher, provider of game and, when necessary, sometime waiter on tables, bed-maker and launderer. He did a mountain of work for next-to-nothing and loved doing it as much as he had come to love the two women who employed and underpaid him for his labours.

"How's Arch?" asked Les, handing Bruno a can of lager.

"As ever," said Bruno.

"Picked up a cheap tape of *Butterfly*, but it's not Callas, when I was up in the city last week." Ray pointed, "Take him that."

"Thanks," said Bruno. "Guess I'll get to hear it five thousand times."

"School going to be all right?" asked Les.

"Dunno," said Bruno quietly. "Guess it's a toss-up." The two women said nothing, looking at him, waiting for him to continue. "It's a struggle, and I know it. Gotta get good enough marks for varsity. Just don't know if I can do it. It's a bitch, really." He chewed his bottom lip. "Should've told old Hassall, when I first went back, that I needed to start right over and not half way through."

"That's not quite right, Bruno," said Ray. "Your marks have been reasonable up till now. Maybe not spectacular. You'll do it. I know — *we* know you will," she said, looking at Lesley.

"Any way we can help?" asked Les.

Bruno took a swig from his can and looked out the window. "Reckon not." Suddenly he smiled and his whole face lit up and livened. "Just feeling sorry for myself," he laughed. "I'll do it. If it's the last thing I do, I'll do it." Another laugh. "And it won't be the last thing I do, either."

"Right on, man," said Ray. "Cheers!" She raised her can of lager.

"This Maori's gonna show 'em he can do more'n hold a Stop–Go sign on the road works," he said, at which all three of them broke into gales of laughter, opened another three cans and didn't stop chuckling for some moments. "This Maori couldn't even do that right," hooted Lesley, and they all laughed again.

"Worst Stop–Go Maori in the whole wide world," said Ray, and they went on laughing.

"Oh, I dunno," said Bruno. "Stopped quite a lot of things, eh?" and he slapped Ray on the back. "Anyway, I better be going. Gotta see to Arch." He tilted his can to his lips and guzzled the remainder. "Needed that. See you two at the weekend."

As a crow is reckoned to fly it was about two kilometres from his home at the top of the hills to the Lodge at the bottom. By track it was almost twice as far. On a good day, and when the bike started, the downhill trip from house to Lodge took about twenty minutes. The return trip took longer and was always a struggle.

"Been outside today, Arch?"

"No," replied his father. "Why should I go outside? To the best of my knowledge we do have indoor plumbing."

"You know what the doctor said," Bruno sighed.

"Bugger the doctor," said the old man. "I sat on the porch."

"That's not exercise, Arch. Sitting on the porch is no exercise at all."

"When you get to my age, you exercise when you want to. When you're seventy-eight and . . ."

"Feeling sorry for yourself, Arch? Come on, old man, we'll walk round the garden together. I don't give a stuff if you're seventy-eight or a-hundred-and-seventy-eight, you're as fit as a fiddle and a buck rat."

"Which one?" His father sniffed. "There's a

monumental difference between the two — or maybe you hadn't noticed."

"Don't you get smart with me, Archibald. Come on." Bruno took his father's arm. "Then I'll do us some eggs."

It was both garden and jungle. Windswept hilltop. Gnarled and wind-bent growth, a garden of no design but of significant, haphazard character. "Find the golden lilies, boy. Should be out about now. I want to see the golden lilies," Arch directed.

Bruno looked down at his father and his mouth twisted in a slight grimace. He said nothing but held his father's arm more firmly.

"Other side of the hydrangeas, boy, and if you don't give them some water . . . Just through here . . ." The old man sniffed at the air. "They're out!" he exclaimed, pushing away from his son, brushing aside the summer growth and the plants he wanted. "See! They are out. I told you," and he buried his face in the overpowering fragrance of the blooms that stood as tall as he.

Bruno laughed. "You got a yellow face, Arch. You got a yellow face from all the pollen."

"Leave me be, boy. You go and do those eggs and leave me here. I planted them. I planted these lilies. Hah! 'Consider the lilies of the field . . .' Yes, well, these ones definitely do not toil, spin, nor do they do anything other than grow. I'll just sit awhile and toil at weeding around them and they may even grow a little more. You do those eggs. Go on, away with you."

It was the beginning of the third week of the new school year before Bruno Petrie had cause to use the senior commonroom in order to sort out the oddities of his own timetable. Generally he steered well clear of the place. He wasn't at school to socialise. As an adult student all he had to do was turn up when he had a class. As luck would have it, and if he could straighten things out, this year it looked as if he'd only have to get into town to school on four days out of the five. A first-rate bonus, if that really were the case. One day up his sleeve just might make all the difference.

He looked up as the door opened and Beth Paterson walked in. He nodded slightly and said an absent-minded, "Hi," and bent back to his work, pen clenched in his teeth. Beth scarcely noticed him, fished a crumpled sweatshirt from her bag and put it on. A midsummer lull; a cool day.

"Lord, you're hard to track down, woman!" Beth's new firm and fast friend, Brenda, came in the door after her. "Anyone'd think you were trying to avoid me." She ignored Bruno and flopped into a chair. "Make me a coffee, there's a good girl," and then she noticed Bruno. "You want one, Bruno?"

Bruno shook his head and started to pack away his gear. What was the use in trying to get anything done in here?

Brenda did not pause for breath. "Party. Saturday. Out at Jenkins'. They got that big farm out towards the saddle. Want you to come. Nick Jenkins said you had to and he's sure one hunk — he was here last year until they kicked him out for doing just about everything . . ."

Beth was saved by the door and the diversion of a fun-fight in the corridor outside. The door was pushed open and one of those on the other side pushed Vic Witt into the commonroom and slammed the door shut on him. Not noticing who was in the room, Vic turned back to the door and fist hammered it, yelling abuse through to his assailant. Then he re-opened the door. No one there. "Whew!" He brushed back his hair and turned into the room, noticing for the first time who was there.

Much later, on reflection, Beth thought that it was probably the best-quality mime she had ever seen. Bruno, standing, picked up his bag, looked straight at Vic, smiled a full, wide smile, and then he winked.

Vic stopped stock still. He gulped, swallowed and blinked before saying, "Erg . . ." followed by another gulp or two.

Brenda, fascinated, darted looks between one and then the other, but said nothing. She sensed there was something going on here and wrinkled her forehead in a concentrated fashion trying to work out what that something was.

Beth caught the white flash of Bruno's teeth and saw the colour draining from Vic's face and suddenly knew who Bruno was.

Vic turned on his heel and fled the room. Bruno walked out after him, zipping up his bag as he walked and whistling tunelessly.

"Well, well, well, well, well!" said Brenda. "Did

you see that, or did you see that? I wonder what it was all about?"

"Who's the big Maori guy?" asked Beth in a dead flat voice as she made coffee for Brenda. "Haven't seen him much round here before except up the back in some of our classes."

"Bruno. Bruno Petrie. You don't see him much. He's an adult student, only old Hassall knows why, and I just bet Petrie threatened him. He shouldn't be allowed back here in the first place. He's not all that much older'n any of us and he's bad news. You name it and he's done it. They should never have let him back — he's violent."

"Where does he live?" asked Beth, even more flatly and quietly.

Brenda looked at Beth and Beth knew she had asked one question too many. "Out by you. You must've seen him. He's got an old motorbike he rides and you see him with a gun over his shoulder," she shuddered. "Up that old road just before Stella's, right up the top. Lives with his old man who's half loopy or dead or something. God knows why he came back to school. You'd never guess what he did when he was here last time . . ."

Beth said nothing and knew she'd soon find out.

"We had this real slime as principal before old Hassall and he's not much better. Well, they're all slime. Got to be to want a job like that, if you ask me. Gonzo, we called him. He knocked him out."

"Who did?" Beth needed some help.

"Bruno Petrie, dummy," Brenda sighed. "And he

was only fourteen. He belted up Gonzo when Gonzo tried to belt him up. Knocked him out and then stuck the boot in and kicked real, real hard. And then he never came back."

"Gonzo?"

"No, thickhead. Bruno never came back. No one ever saw him again until all of a sudden he turned up last year or it might have been the year before and came back to school. I bet he threatened old Hassall with the same treatment as poor old Gonzo got. Talk about aggro. Wow! Bad, bad, bad. I reckon Vic Witt's a pussycat's kitten compared to Bruno Petrie and I just wonder what's up between those two . . ."

"How's your timetable?" Beth changed the subject.

"It's great. I don't do nothing for half the week. How's yours?"

"Impossible." Beth was looking through the open door.

Chapter 7

She had walked up the road before. Indeed, she thought she had walked its full length. Calling the dirt track a road was certainly stretching it a bit. Once upon a time it might have been metalled and maintained but that time had long past.

It didn't even have a name. Well, not a proper name.

"No-name Road, honey. That's what they call it. That's its name," said Stella.

"It hasn't got a name?"

"It's No-name Road, that's its name. Why? You look on a map, there's one somewhere around here." Her aunt cast vaguely around and finally ended up pointing at a dresser.

"I don't need a map," said Beth. "I just wanted to know about it. I walk up it."

"It's about three miles to the top, hon. Nice walk and glorious views," said Stella. "Haven't done it in years."

"I've only been a bit of the way, then. Maybe half. I thought it stopped when it hit the stream."

"The old ford."

"I reckon," said Beth. "Does anyone live on it? The road?"

"Right up the very top. There's an old roadman's cottage from the early days when they did bother to keep it up. I think there were several farms along it back then. Nothing now. God knows what happened. Land round here's no good for farming, that's likely what happened."

"Who lives there?"

"Old Arch Petrie did. I think he's still there. Never did see much of him. You must have seen his son at school. The gorgeous Bruno. God, I'd kill for a head of hair like his — and those wonderful teeth! He's had his moments, has Bruno. Maybe you haven't seen him yet. Mature student, and might not have started. Doesn't have to turn up for all the nonsense you little kids do," Stella laughed. "How's it going? Bit of a change, eh?"

"It's okay."

"Yes, well, I guess you'll survive your stint at Gray's Valley High. Countless others have. Endured might be the better word. It's no great hall of ivy but it's not all that bad."

"If I can ever come to grips with my timetable," Beth sighed.

Her aunt laughed. "Don't expect the impossible, honey. No one else has ever mastered them. Since poor old Harry fell in love with a computer nothing's been straight. Want me to sort it out for you?"

"No, no," said Beth hastily. "It's falling into place. Almost got it sorted out."

The following Sunday Beth sat at the ford for half an hour, hunched beneath the overhang of a small rocky outcrop, arms around her legs and chin on her knees. She emptied her mind.

She knew she shouldn't be there. Shouldn't be out. Could ill afford the time. Time wasted?

Maybe it was knowing that the track, the road, went further that drew her on after that half hour. At first she stood and moved as if to climb down the hill, then changed her mind and hesitantly pressed ahead. In midsummer the stream was just a trickle, little more than a muddy pothole, and she jumped from one side to the other.

The road twisted, almost turning back on itself, dropped, climbed higher before dropping again and then, finally, climbed through thickening, over-hanging second-growth bush.

Beth rounded a corner and stopped still, drew breath and did what she could to blend into the shadow of the trees. Two goats, a nanny and her kid, one black and one white, were almost within her reach, delicately feeding on roadside weed and low foliage. She stared, fascinated. Their sudden alarm at some almost imperceptible movement on her part caused her to start. They were there and then they were gone. A bleat and then a flickering of black and white into shadow. Gone. Beth shook her head and walked on into the shade.

Suddenly there was sunlight. The growth thinned and she came out onto a small plateau. The road petered out into a rough, gravelled and grassed clearing on the far side of which, facing away from the road, stood a house. The whole place was unfenced and the building sat in a wilderness of half scrub and half garden. A lean-to porch with door beyond and one window was all that could be seen from the road. The whole structure was of grey, weathered, corrugated iron. It was unpainted.

Beth moved into the clearing and took five, six steps towards the building.

"What d'you want?"

Beth blinked in the sunlight. "Er . . ."

"You lost or something?" Bruno Petrie, barefoot and wearing nothing but a rather too small pair of once white shorts, came round the corner of the house and stood near the porch.

"No. No, I'm not lost," Beth cleared her throat. "I wanted to see what was at the end of the road."

"Now you've seen," said Bruno, and he stared, unblinking, across at her.

"I live down the bottom," she said.

"I know where you live."

"Is someone there, boy?" A voice from within the house.

"No one, Arch," said Bruno, staring straight at Beth and not raising his voice.

"I can hear someone, boy"

"It's nothing, Arch." Bruno did not take his eyes off Beth.

"Why are you lying?" asked Beth.

"You've seen what's here. There's nothing more," said Bruno, starting to turn away.

The back door creaked open. "I know there's someone here. I can hear voices, dammit, and they're not all in my head."

"Good — good afternoon, Mr er . . . Petrie."

"Knew I was right. You the District Nurse? Bugger off if you are."

Bruno's eyes were hard and the corners of his mouth turned down. "Arch, this is . . . I don't know her name . . ."

"Beth. Beth Paterson."

"She lives with Stella Gordon," said Bruno.

"That batty art woman?" Arch Petrie held out a hand. "Pleased to meet you, girl. Come here."

Beth did not move.

"This is my father, Arch Petrie," said Bruno. "And don't just stand there," — a sneer on his face and in his voice — "can't you see he's blind?"

Beth stared first at the son and then at the father. Then she walked over to the old man and took his hand. "And I'm pleased to meet you, Mr Petrie," she said. "I'm sorry I disturbed you and your son. I'll go now. The other thing I came for was to say thank you to your son."

"God knows what for," said Arch. "Precious little I ever had to thank him for. Thank him for what?"

"He, er . . . Bruno, well, he sort of rescued me from a bad situation a couple of weeks back and I didn't know who he was. He was wearing a hat pulled down over his head and his face. I've, well, sort of just found out." Beth wished she could stop talking and that the old man would stop shaking her hand and the old man's son would take his jeering and cruel eyes off her.

"Come inside, girl. Bruno will make us some tea. Get the silver pot out, Bruno," Arch said, wiping the sneer from the face of his son. "Not every day we have a visitor. Not every year we have a young, and I'm sure attractive, woman come to call. Now come inside and tell me all about my young Sir Galahad."

Sir Galahad, jeerless, gritted his teeth and followed the other two into the house.

Nothing prepared her for what she saw. The almost hovel-like back porch and its boots, sticks, boxes, sacks and old coats led directly into a central kitchen and dining area with a doorway leading off at each side. A further doorway, straight ahead, led into one of the most beautiful rooms she had ever seen. It ran the whole width of the building and may once have been two or three smaller rooms. It was the grace of the place, the style, rather than any extravagance, that struck Beth. The walls were painted a soft cream, very plain. The windows of three sides of the room were hung with heavy drapes of velvet. There was evidence that they had once been a deep sky-blue but had faded over the many years they had hung. The floor was wooden, uncarpeted except for one or two old rugs. The furniture was basic, worn, but of good design.

It was what lay beyond the room, rather than anything in the room itself, that took the breath away. Through a trio of almost floor to ceiling windows could be seen row upon row of hills, mountains. Rather than loom above the house they seemed to drop away from it in ragged, serried ranks of greens, greys, blues and purples to a far horizon of pale sky beyond.

"Surprised?" the old man chuckled. "I can always tell. Sit down."

"It's incredible, Mr Petrie," said Beth. "You just get no idea, no idea at all when you come up that road."

"True," said Arch. "And that's probably why it seems more than it really is when you first see it. Mind you, I never tire of looking at it." He smiled. Beth said nothing. "And I still do see it, you know," he guessed into her silence. "The mind's eye. A powerful optic, that."

"Yes," she said.

Bruno, silent, made tea. Quickly, neatly and efficiently.

"Is much of that land out there yours?" she asked.

"Most of what you can see, my dear," the man waved a hand. "Three thousand acres, or whatever it is we're supposed to call it these days."

"Hectares," grunted Bruno, placing his father's tea on a small table and guiding Arch's hand towards it. "Twelve or thirteen hundred of them. That's our estate, isn't it, Arch?" he added, an edge to his voice.

"Do — d'you run, what? Sheep? Cows?" she asked.

"Cattle, I think you mean," said Bruno. "No. Well, that's not quite true. We still have some sheep, don't we, Arch? Like about six?" Again an edge.

The father overrode the son. "It was my every intention when I bought this place some thirty years back that the bulk of it be allowed to revert to bush. Marginal farming. Marginal."

53

"Not quite as marginal as we've made it," muttered Bruno.

She finished her tea and rose to leave. The old man fascinated her and she would like to have stayed and enjoyed his company and his old-fashioned courtesy. She knew she would be welcome. But from the other, the son — son? — the complete absence of any welcome, much less warmth, was perfectly clear. Beth made her excuses.

"It's dark," said Arch. Beth did not contradict him. "I know when it's dark, my dear. The boy will walk you to the ford." He raised a hand. "Don't protest, either of you," he said and gave a small smile. "Come again, girl. There's not much to talk to round here."

"I can find my own way," Beth said, once they were clear of the house.

"I'll do as I'm told," Bruno replied sharply.

They walked in silence for a couple of minutes.

"You've got some goats out on the road just up here. I saw them and then they saw me and ran. There was a black one and a little wee white one."

"Thanks," he said. "I'll take the rifle tomorrow and get them."

"What?" she sounded surprised.

"Well, it's never going to revert to bush like the old man wants, not with those sods around." He took a sideways glance at her, assessing the effect of his words.

"I—I just thought you might farm them," said Beth.

"They're wild. Well, they're half wild," said Bruno. "Problem is, Arch loves his second-growth bush, plus every pest that moves in it." He kept an eye on her. "Talk about a contradiction and a quandary. It's in defiance of all logic."

"Huh?" said Beth.

Bruno stopped in the half light of the roadway and Beth turned towards him. "Well, I am my father's son," he said. Then he smiled and then he laughed. "What sort of thing did you expect me to say?"

Beth shook her head and remembered her aunt's description of Bruno. Without the snigger, the sneer or the sulky jeer he was a different person. "Guess that's one way to put it. But, search me, I don't know whether it defies all logic or not. Anyway, here's the ford. Thanks and goodbye." She stepped quickly across the mud.

"Hey!" he called after her.

"What?" She stopped and looked back.

"Well," and he paused. "I'm sorry . . . you know . . ."

"No. I don't know. What for?" Let him sweat it out.

He grinned across at her. "For being a bit of a dickhead, that's what," and he turned back up the road.

She let him go a few paces. "Hey!" she called after him.

"What?" He stopped.

"Is it right you knocked out the principal at school and then stuck your boot in?"

"Huh . . . huh?"

"Well, is it?" She could see him move in the dark.

"Mind your own business," he laughed.

She stayed listening to him laughing well into the distance, then she turned and walked briskly down the road to Stella's house. Her arms swung freely at her side.

Chapter 8

Bruno gave little thought to Beth in the weeks that followed. Even had he wanted to, there was no time. Time; the one thing he was ever short of. The one commodity that ran out quicker than Arch's whisky.

Time to get his father to the doctor for his three-month checkup, and he could never do that unless Les and Ray lent him the Jeep. Time to get Arch down to the specialist, the ophthalmologist, and the usual, no-hope diagnosis. Then the time to catch up on the missed days of school. Read. Read. Read.

Time to get the oval rockgarden finished outside the Lodge in time for autumn planting. Back-breaking work, going too fast just to get it done. Time to serve the needs of the twelve Japanese guests when Ray came down with a summer 'flu. Time to keep their freezer full.

Shopping. A bit of housework. Cooking. Time for just sitting with his father. Too little time for the old man.

What time, then, for English, history, maths and all the others? Far too little.

If only he had a decent vehicle. Anything. Bike, car, truck. Anything that went. Just something that would get him from one place to another, not necessarily with time to spare, but, for a change, on time. The old motorbike, when it went, was good enough to get him up and down No-name but certainly not from the crossroads to the town. And that was the major hassle. There were only two buses a day, neither at the right time and seldom running to schedule. That generally meant hitching, and it surely wasn't the busiest state highway in the world. An hour's walk was often the order of the day, both morning and afternoon, and time had to be allowed for this.

Early autumn. A first frost and the bike wouldn't start. He had jogged the road, no great problem, then fluked a lucky hitch. He had been to school and then shopped for what he and Arch needed, hitched yet again and finally walked up his road. No hint of frost now; Indian summer hot. Bruno sweated. He was tired and bad-tempered.

"To hell with it!" was all he said, throwing his pack down. He stripped off his damp sweatshirt, flung himself into the warm dry grass and went to sleep.

At first, when he awoke he couldn't place where he was. He sat up, shook his head and then he remembered. Bruno glanced at his watch and shrugged and reached for his pack. He opened the small front pouch, fished around for his cigarettes and lighter, lit one, lay back down and day-dreamed.

"Feel better?" The voice came from above him.

He did not look up. "If that's you, God, the answer's no and all you've done is make me waste two hours."

"Damn. I thought I'd frighten you," Beth slipped from the rock where she had been sitting for some minutes and crouched down near Bruno.

"Last time anything frightened me on this road I must've been three years old," said Bruno. He sat up. "No. You can't be God. God's a black woman. I read that somewhere."

"How's your father?"

"Dunno. He was all right this morning. Instead of spying on me you could've gone up and seen him. You know where he lives and you've never been back . . ." A slight sneer. He shook his head again. "Sorry. Just I'm a bit tired."

She did not know what to say. "Yeah."

He winked at her. "Life's a bitch."

She smiled at him. "So I've heard."

"And so's my motorbike. That's why I'm sitting here now."

"What's wrong with it?" Beth asked.

"Dunno. Wouldn't start this morning."

"Did it have any gas in it?" she asked.

"Good point," he looked at her. "The one thing I didn't check. It's clapped out, anyway. Old as the hills, and it's these hills that wrecked it. All I want is for it to go."

"It'll go if you look after it. Even if it is old," she said seriously.

Bruno turned to her. "What would you know about it?"

"More than you'd think," she said.

"Go on."

"Well . . ." Now she was unsure. "See, I had this scooter back—back home. Bought it with my baby-sitting money. Just about as old as your hills, too."

"So?"

"Mum didn't want me to get it. I sure had no money to get it fixed if it broke down, so I went to these night classes. Motorbike maintenance for teenagers. Once a week for about three months, a term. There were these thirteen guys, who thought they knew everything, and there was me."

"Good on you," said Bruno.

"D'you know how your bike works?"

"Yep," he said.

"Honest?"

"Nope."

"Like me to have a look at it?"

"Why?"

"It could help, and you sure need it — the bike, I mean."

"It's only an old farm bike," said Bruno.

"So? It's a bike," said Beth. "And as far as I know, it's the only one you've got."

It was his turn to be unsure. "Why?" was all he could say.

Beth looked at him, still uncertain. She chose her words carefully. "I—I'd like to help. You helped me out a while back . . ." She paused and looked at him. He was about to say something and she could see the beginnings of a sneer curl into the corners of his mouth. Her words came quickly. "I reckon I've got a bit more time than you have. Look, anyone can see you're rushed off your feet. School, and your dad, and your jobs and all that. I'm not blind, and don't think I've been spying and nosing around. I haven't. Actually I haven't got all that much time either, but I think I've got more than you and I'd have to be dead thick not to notice we're both having a bit of a struggle at school. Even Brenda Macaulay's doing better than us, and that's after spending half the day on her hair and the other half on her fingernails. I know that's a bit unfair. . ."

"Shoot!" he said, and grinned at her.

"Well?"

"Well what? If you can do anything with my bike you're welcome to have a go. And if you can get it going I'll change my mind about God being a black lady."

"Nice girl, is she?" Ray looked at Les and winked.

"What d'you mean?" Bruno picked up his coffee mug and took a swallow, avoiding their eyes.

"Plain as the nose on my face," said Les to Ray.

"What are you talking about?" asked Bruno.

"Nothing. Nothing at all," said Les.

"Certainly a paragon of all mechanical virtues," said Ray. "Well, Bruno, from what you say, she must be."

"You're having me on," Bruno looked between the two of them.

"And the bike's still going?" asked Ray.

"It's like I told you," said Bruno patiently. "She gave it a complete overhaul and got one or two bits and pieces and even found one or two more things in the shed amongst the stuff I got when I first bought it. It's as good as new. Brilliant."

"Who is she, this mechanic of yours?" asked Ray.

"Beth," he said. "I told you."

"It's that rather nice art teacher's niece. Stella something. They were talking about her in the library when I was in there last week," said Lesley. "Lives in that old converted schoolhouse up at the crossroads. You know the one. Did it up herself, I'm told. Whole conversion. Nice job, too."

"Must run in the family," said Ray. "Being practical, that is. It must do."

"You two are teasing me," said Bruno, "I can tell."

"Heaven forbid we'd ever do that," said Ray. "Tell you what, my fine-feathered Bruno, bring her round for dinner one night when we haven't got anyone in. She might even take a look at the Jeep for us. Needs a bit of work and a tune-up. And you can bring dinner . . . which reminds me, there's a party of Swedes or Scandinavians or somesuch . . ."

"No, no, no, no, no . . ." Bruno threw up his hands.

"If you like, I'll have a go at the brakes, and you sure need lights. Then it'd be good enough for a warrant and you could ride it right into town and to school. You'd have to get it registered, though," Beth told Bruno.

"Be no good," he grinned.

"Why not?" Beth asked.

"Haven't got a licence to drive the thing!"

"Doesn't stop you buzzing round here."

"That's different. Like, what cop's ever gonna drive up No-name? And I can ride it on the farm, no sweat. That's okay. Only time I could get caught is if I've been at the Lodge at night and then come home round the gorge instead of up the farm. But it's always late and no one'd see me, anyway. Not without lights," he grinned and looked at the machine. "It's great. It's saved me heaps. Heaps of time, most of all."

"Good," she said. They had been together on one of the two buses of the day out of town. They stood, still a little wary in each other's company. Not quite knowing what to say and not quite knowing how to part. Bruno moved to drag his bike further from the patch of scrub on the crossroads where he parked it.

"Better get going," he said, and straddled the bike.

"Come and have a cup of tea," invited Beth, "at Stella's. She's not home, and you caught the bus so you've got plenty of time and—and . . . come ·and have a cup of tea." Why was it, she thought, that she couldn't stop soon enough whenever she said anything to him? Why was it that, once she got going, she always said too much?

"Okay," he said, holding up a hand, "okay." He smiled at her. "I'd like one. Thanks."

"And you've gotta buy a safety helmet," she said, as she led the way.

"What a mess! What a great mess!" He looked around Stella's living room and laughed. "It's a bit like her, eh? It's the sort of room you'd imagine old

Stella to have. How on earth can she ever find anything?"

"She never does," said Beth. "And don't be rude. All because you live in perfect neatness with everything in its place and you're obviously the world's best housekeeper . . ."

"I am not," he broke in, suddenly serious. "We lived in the middle of a whole heap of junk, but I had to toss it all away, get rid of it, when Arch went blind. Just had to. It's obvious."

"How long ago was that?" she asked.

"Couple of years. Bit longer, maybe."

"What happened? Like, how did he go blind?"

"Am I allowed to smoke in here?" Bruno asked.

"No way," she said. "Oh, all right, go on. Probably no worse a health hazard than the stink of Stella's turpentine and paints. You can open all the windows."

Bruno lit a cigarette. "He went over that bluff just before the bush where you saw those goats."

"Fell? Did he fall over there?"

"In a way. We had a van. Had it for years. And if you think my motorbike was a mess . . . Fridays, Arch'd go into town and do whatever he had to do, buy food and stuff. Then, more often than not, he'd get blind, stinking, paralytic drunk at the pub. Sometimes he'd be so bad they'd keep him there. This wasn't one of those times and he didn't quite make it home. I didn't find him till the next day. Not a scratch on him but he'd knocked his head. The nerves in behind his eyes — the optic somethings — they got shattered. That was it. That was all, except he was half-drowned in his own spew." The corners of Bruno's mouth turned down again. "So," — he spread his hands — "it's me'n Arch. Well, it always was. Guess it always will be until . . . I look after the old devil."

"I think you do it very well," said Beth, and cast around in her mind for something else to say. She came up with the wrong catch. "Well . . . what about your mother?"

He stood, stubbed out his cigarette and said, "Better be going," his mouth well down.

Beth swallowed. "Sorry. I—I didn't mean to be nosy," then her temper rose. "But why, for God's sake, d'you have to be so prickly? It was an ordinary question."

Bruno looked at her for a moment and then sat down again. He did not take his eyes from hers. "My mother died when I was three. I don't remember her. That was a car smash, too. Arch married her when he was nearly an old man. One of his boozing Fridays he picked her up out of the gutter outside the pub in town, the Criterion. She was dead drunk and she'd been beaten up real bad. She'd been with a shearing gang . . ."

Beth started to say something but Bruno stopped her. "You asked," he reminded her. "Arch took her home. Why? Dunno. She stayed. Stayed for about three years and looked after him. Somewhere along the line she did something more than cook and housekeep and she got pregnant with me. Arch, being Arch, married her. Two years after that she took off with a fencer. Reckon it must've been the last time

Arch ever had any fencing done on the place. Then, some time later, one day the cops came out and told Arch her and the fencer got wasted in a car smash." Bruno spread his hands again. "That's it. End of story."

"I am sorry I asked," said Beth.

"No you're not," he said.

"Was . . . was she a Maori?" Beth asked.

First he just smiled at her and then he laughed out loud. "Sure was," he laughed. "Can't you tell?" More laughter. "I don't think it's a crime. Well . . ." he drawled out the word, "maybe it is. Yep, Eleanor Smith, she was a Maori. That's my mother. She was about half Maori according to Arch, although I don't know how he checked. She'd had a knock on the head as a kid and Arch said she was just a little bit simple."

Beth smiled at him. "Well, she must've been to have had you."

"Hey! That's not nice."

"Have you got relations on her side, your mother's side?" she asked.

This time his mouth turned right down. "God knows," he said, shortly. "I sure don't know. No one ever knew where she came from and Eleanor Smith might not've been her real name. Arch said he did everything he could to find out. For my sake, see. Just nothing, nothing at all."

"It's sad," said Beth.

"Like hell it is," said Bruno. "It's just ordinary and you're the first person — the *very* first person — I ever, ever told."

66

Beth tried to lighten his mood. "Well, I reckon Eleanor Smith must have been quite nice looking," she said.

"How would you know?" he asked.

"Because you look nothing like your father," she said.

"That's a bit hard to tell," said Bruno. "He's seventy-eight and I'm nineteen. He could've looked just like me, only whiter," he smiled.

Time to even a few scores. "I reckon you're just about the best-looking guy I've seen for ages." Beth kept smiling.

"Huh?" said Bruno.

"And I don't think you even know it," she ploughed on. "And if you weren't so dark skinned I think you'd be blushing. How about another cup of tea?"

"You're just trying to embarrass me, and I don't want any more tea," said Bruno.

"Sure am," said Beth.

"Still," he shrugged, "that's cool. Must remind me to have a look next time I have a shave — except that the mirror's cracked and we only got one."

She looked at him; blue-black hair and eyes so brown they were almost black. The whole of his face came alive when he smiled. Only he didn't seem to smile too often.

"Not that it matters a damn," Beth shrugged. "Doesn't matter a damn how anyone looks."

"That's great," he said. "You build a guy up and then you chop him down."

"That's life," said Beth.

"Yeah, and there won't be any life for me if I don't get home and get some work done. And don't think you're off the hook, woman. You dig into my history, I'm gonna dig into yours. Yeah. Why're you living here with old Stella? Fair's fair."

"Old Stella? *Old* Stella?" Neither had heard Stella Gordon come in. "What's this about old Stella? Tell me about it."

"Sorry, Miss Gordon," Bruno stood. "Just going."

"Really? What a pity. I come home to find a handsome young man in my house and he walks out on me before I've even had time to sit down. Story of my life."

Beth and Bruno laughed loudly.

Chapter 9

She still walked. Most evenings, regardless of the weather. It was well into autumn now, and colder, often drizzling, damp. These days Mt Gray was not often seen, or else it seemingly hung suspended in a wisping warp and weft of smoky mist. There one minute and gone the next. Mists that would shrug from the mountain down into and through the gorge and up into the smaller valleys.

The ache and unease within her, Beth thought, was not unlike the fogs that drifted in, settled a while and then passed on. The warmth of Stella's house and her company could ease things momentarily. So, too, the casual, chance relationships she built up at school. The moments with Bruno? Well, they were little more than that; snatched conversations if they shared a class at school, if they caught the same bus, if she happened across him at the intersection of the highway and No-name Road. She did not seek him out. She sought no one.

School was not going well. It wasn't hard for her to work out why. Quite simply, she was doing too little work.

Brenda noticed. "Look, girl, this junk should be

a piece of cake to you. You're light years brighter'n me. What's up?"

"Can't be bothered, I s'pose" said Beth. They sipped the lukewarm coffee that was Brenda's specialty. "Dunno, really. Just can't get into it."

Brenda looked at Beth and spoke slowly. "If there's anything you ever want to talk about, need to talk about — you know — I'd listen."

"Why is it everyone always thinks that talking about something makes it better — makes it go away," Beth snapped. "Talking only brings things up that should stay down." She looked at Brenda. "Hey, I'm sorry," she said, managing a smile. "Thanks, anyway."

Brenda took no notice of Beth's outburst. "I mean it. You can snap my thick head off as much as you like and I'm gonna have a growl at you, anyway."

Beth lightened, threw up her hands in pretend horror. "I give up. I surrender. What have I done? Well, that's my problem, eh? I've done nothing."

"That's just about it. You don't go anywhere. You don't see anyone. Nothing. And, now — here goes — you're getting far too friendly with Bruno Petrie. Don't think I haven't noticed that. I have warned you."

"I don't know what you mean," said Beth.

"You do so know. Look, kid, he's bad news, that one, and I don't care if he does look like some brown god and if anyone knocks him on the head — and it's bound to happen sooner or later — I want first grab at his eyelashes. He's bad news. By bad, I mean *bad*."

"It's years since he booted the principal, and I still

don't know what you mean. We just say hello. That's really about all," said Beth.

"You can tell that to the birds, but not to me," said Brenda. "You can't fool me when it comes to these things. Look, booting old Gonzo wasn't all he did. For starters, he booted anything that moved. Talk about wild! What didn't move he chopped down or nicked. Then, after he nearly took old Gonzo to the cleaners or sent him to heaven, or wherever teachers go, he took off . . ."

"I don't want to know," said Beth. "Really, Brenda, I don't know him and I don't suppose I ever will."

"Well, you're going to know. It's for your own good. Anyway, he took off to Auckland and he ran wild there, absolutely wild, for about two years," said Brenda, nodding vigorously as if in some way underlining the accuracy of her information.

"So? Thousands do," said Beth.

"Not just wild. Wild! Wild! Wild!"

"What on earth do you mean?" Beth sighed. Whether she wanted to hear all this or not it was clear Brenda was going to tell her.

"I don't know the whole story. But what I do know I got from this guy when I stayed up with my cousin about a year ago, might be longer, but it wasn't long after when Bruno Petrie came back because things got far too hot for him up there. Seems that big bad Bruno became a sort of king of the streets. Boss of a whole gang of street kids and not just the nice glue sniffers but the vicious ones. Thieves, muggers, druggies, whatever. You think of it and Petrie was in the middle of it. It's the truth. They'd do cars. They'd do—do anything. Like real evil."

"I don't believe it," said Beth.

"It is the truth," said Brenda, seriously. "They'd do little old grandmas for their handbags. Not a pretty sight," she shook her head. "This guy, he even told me they wasted — that means killed — one or two of their own gang, their own mates, who weren't towing the line. Not very sweet at all." Brenda shook her head again. "This guy said don't ever, ever tell anyone anything of this otherwise it might get tracked back to him because he'd sort of been in on the fringes and he didn't want to end up tossed over a motorway bridge in the middle of the night." Brenda stared hard at Beth. "You're the only one I've ever told. Honest. And I'm only telling you for your own sake. What really puzzles me is why the hell is Bruno Petrie back here and what's he got planned? He scares me." She shivered. "It's those eyes."

"I thought you wanted his lashes."

"I'm not joking, kid," said Brenda.

Beth gave a short laugh. "No, but you've been watching too much junk telly or videos. Seems to me, for a big-time hood he's going to a mountain of trouble and pain setting himself up locally. There can't be all that many grandmas to mug in Gray's Valley."

"Laugh your silly head off then," said Brenda. "You'll see. It's all a cover. What's he busy growing on his mad, flakey father's farm, if he hasn't bopped him off already, tell me that?"

"Well I don't know, do I? I'll ask him," said Beth.

"God almighty, don't do that." Brenda shuddered dramatically. "Look, forget what I said. I've said too much already. Just forget it, but remember I warned you."

"I'll make us a cup of coffee, Brenda. You're losing your marbles. You really are. For one thing, it's going to be very hard to forget what you told me and then remember what you warned me about!"

"Smart tart! Here's poor old Vic. He looks so run down, they must have sorted out his timetable. Try to be nice to him. He's not all bad or a mad rapist even though he tries to be. Offer to make him a cup of coffee. You can't hold grudges forever and if you can see some good in Bruno Petrie you must see old Vic's just about a saint."

"Coffee, Vic?" asked Beth, before he had a chance to back out the door.

"Er ... yeah. Thanks," said Vic.

"I made you a cake, Mr Petrie." Now she wished she hadn't. The only good thing about the gesture was that Arch wouldn't have to see the lopsided effort. She hoped it tasted better than it looked. "It's a chocolate one and there are walnuts on top of it." It had seemed a good idea. Like, what else do you take for someone who gets out a silver teapot for afternoon tea? It was only the second cake she had ever made. She turned down the ghetto blaster on Maria Callas.

"Ladies a plate," Arch smiled. "Bruno's out."

"I know."

"Chasing some poor defenceless creature for those

two dames who run that lodge. Nuttier than the walnuts on your cake, those two. Nuttier than your aunt, from what I hear. Scrape them off my slice. They get under my plate."

"Eh?"

"The walnuts. They're no good with dentures," said Arch.

She set about making tea, and warmed the silver pot. Arch had followed her through to the kitchen. In the confines of his home it was hard to tell that he was blind. "You don't like hunting, Mr Petrie?" She looked into the clear, pale blue eyes that did not appear sightless.

"No." He paused for a moment. "There's enough killing and bloodshed on this ridiculous planet of ours without my own flesh and blood adding to it."

"What he catches gets used though," said Beth, pouring the boiling water into the pot. She looked again at the old man as he hovered between the two rooms. She thought he looked more frail than when she had last seen him. "It's all ready. I'll bring it through."

"Too much killing. They do no harm, the things he chases, poor souls. They do no harm but I can't stop him." He did not move from the doorway. "There is no need for us to eat flesh. I haven't eaten meat for God knows how long. Vile stuff! Putrefying muscle tissue of dead animals. Pah!"

"I'm bringing the tea things through," she repeated, and watched him move towards his chair. She poured his cup and placed it by his hand as she had seen

74

Bruno do. She picked the rather large chunks of walnut from his slice of the cake, thinking that they were probably far too big to affect his dentures, anyway.

"Defenceless beasts. God knows they deserve better in their final moments than the sight of my son grinning down upon them. Blood lust is all it is."

"How's the cake?"

"What's that? Oh yes. The cake. I do go on, don't I? The cake? Scrumptious. Longer than I care to remember since anyone made me a cake. You shouldn't have bothered."

"It was no bother," she lied, hoping she got back to Stella's kitchen before Stella did.

"A grave pity my son didn't make a cake or two rather than blasting the hell out of wretched animals," Arch continued. "Much better for him." He gave a little chuckle. "And for me, too. Such a long way for you to come, girl."

"I felt like a walk." This was the truth. "And it's so beautiful, so very beautiful up here."

"It is that, girl."

"Is that why you came to live here in the first place?" Beth asked.

"In part, yes. Of course it is. This spot, this magic spot . . . cast a spell on me the first time I saw it. I may have told you that before."

The put-put of the motorbike could be heard as it climbed towards the house. "Here's Bruno," she said.

"Unlikely to be anyone else, child. Used to be others. Wretched youths on their bikes out for Sunday fun and, as often as not, with guns. Give him his due, my Bruno got rid of all of them. Frightened them all off."

She started. "Did he?"

"Tell me he hasn't caught anything. Have a look, there's a good girl. Please."

She looked. "No. No, he hasn't," she lied again.

"Good." Arch breathed a satisfied sigh.

"Took me an hour to corner that little sucker," Bruno announced as he came in. "Good! Great! Cake? I'm starved."

"You're a nice girl," Arch said quietly. "Too nice, quite likely."

"What was all that about?" Bruno followed Beth to the kitchen.

"Nothing," said Beth. "God, you've got blood all over you."

"It's okay," he smiled. "Arch can't see." He grinned more broadly.

"No, but I can," she said sharply.

"So?" The grin had gone. "I'll give you a lift back down when you're ready to go," he offered.

"I'd rather walk. I like walking. Remember?" She looked at him. "Two new spark plugs in there. They're by the stereo. I got them in town. You owe me."

"You'll have to wait till next week. Broke," said Bruno, carving himself half of the cake. "This looks good."

"If you gave up smoking . . ." she began.

He held up a hand. "Tell me about it. Can't be perfect. It's my only vice."

"Is it?" was all she said.

"Come back here, girl," Arch called. "I want to talk to you. You're not here that often that I can waste the opportunity."

Bruno's eyes were hard and there was no trace of a smile on his face. "I'll walk down to the ford with you," he said. "You're not the only one who likes walking."

"Please yourself," she said.

"Find the tapes of *La Traviata,* girl. Save me endless hours of trying out one after the other. I sometimes suspect that Bruno jumbles them all on purpose. Am I right, lad?"

"Something like that, Arch," said Bruno softly.

"Look, Mr Petrie . . ." she began.

"I just wish I could," said Arch.

"I'm sorry." She wished she could just get up and leave.

"Don't be silly. I shouldn't be such a smart-arse at the expense of others. It's only when you don't see that you suddenly realise how much of our everyday conversation centres around sight. Think about it."

"I will," said Beth. "But what I was going to say was that I reckon I can come up with some sort of Braille-type code so that you can tell your tapes and records by touch."

"I'd never remember it," said Arch. "But it's a nice idea."

"No need to do them all. Just the ones you play over and over again. Like Maria Callas." She smiled.

"You're laughing at me," said Arch. "I can tell. Maria drives poor Bruno out of his mind and often out of the house. I told him once that Callas had died. He said that was probably the only considerate thing she'd ever done. Philistine!"

"I know what that means," said Beth.

Chapter 10

"Bloody hell!" he snarled. "Get off my back, will you? If you lived with him like I've lived with him for all, or most of, my life, you'd bloody need to kill something, too!"

"I —"

Bruno didn't give her a chance. "I tell you what, there are days when I gotta get out of that house, and plugging some animal is better by far than strangling my father." He shook his head. "And I didn't mean that." He looked up. "Or maybe I do."

"Look, I don't care," Beth said. "And I didn't ask you to walk down the road with me. All I was going to say to you was, is there any way you can keep it, well, more away from him?" She was not going to let Bruno get under her skin.

"I do," he said. "Usually I do. All right, it was stupid of me to have said anything when I came in before. Usually I don't . . ." He paused. "Maybe I was doing it just to look big to you. Get it? Big macho hunter?"

"Really?" She sounded surprised.

"Sit down for a minute," he said. "Please?" They sat, almost back-to-back on a rock. "What is it about you that makes me tell you things that I never told anyone else? What do I know about you? Big fat zero. Sweet nothing at all."

"There's nothing much to know," said Beth.

"I'll bet," he said. "Look," he breathed hard. "I'm a Maori, or least part-Maori. I sure look like one more'n I look like anything else. It's big in my head. I guess it has to be. But it's got to be something and nothing, and that's hard. I've got no tribe, no Maori roots other than what you see. And that should count for a helluva lot. And that bit of me that should count for a helluva lot, in the end it can't count for much at all. No tribe, no family, no people.

"I've got nothing but Arch and this hunk of useless land that the old fool bought and that I've come to love, that I do love with every little bit of me. It is me and I am it. It's just about part of my body. I am its trees and gullies and its scrub and its grass. I'm its hares and rabbits and goats and deer and I take from it nothing — nothing that I shouldn't. If I take even a goat, well, I take a little part of me. It is of me. I am of it. Get it?"

"I think so," said Beth.

"I have been part of this place since, well, probably before I could walk. As soon as I could walk I pretty soon got to know it all. There was nothing else. By the time I was seven and Miss Forsythe came for me, I was so much a part of it, it would've taken crowbars and everything to get me off it."

"Miss Forsythe?"

"That house you and Stella live in, she lived there.

It was the schoolhouse. There was a school just along the road at the beginning of the gorge. She taught there forever. When I was seven she came and got me to go to school. Took her a week to catch me, and Arch was no help. Took her another week to get me into sort of reasonable clothes. Then months of chasing me when I wouldn't stay at school. I'd run away . . . sure you want to hear all this?"

"Yes."

"Nine of us in that school. Eight girls and me. I don't think I came across another boy until I went to Gray's Valley High. Well, I guess I must've seen one or two, but that was about it. Now, old Forsythe was not your usual sort of teacher. She only did one thing — she taught us to read. Nothing else. She'd taught there for just so long that no one had the guts to do anything about it — if it mattered, and now I don't think it did. We sure could read. What else is there, really?

"She used to take us for walks. I think she took us for walks whenever she wanted some exercise. Other than that, we did some painting and she sat by the fire in winter and out in the sun in summer. She used to drink tea with whisky in it, just like Arch. She used to smoke all the time, too," he laughed. "I think she must've taught me how to smoke. I don't think she meant to . . ." He stopped.

"Go on," said Beth.

"If I didn't turn up at school, she'd harness up her old car — believe it or not it was a Model-T Ford — and come to get me. Then she'd sit for hours with

Arch drinking more tea and whisky and listening to Maria Callas or whoever. God knows what the girls did when she was up at our place. She sure was old," he laughed. "Then she'd take to me with a piece of supplejack and beat the hell out of me, yelling at the top of her voice, 'I never did believe in corporal punishment but the good Lord knows there's an exception to every rule!' God!"

"Seems you were happy to take from her what you wouldn't take from poor Mr Gonzo," said Beth cautiously.

"Once or twice a year she'd drag me into town, buy me some clothes, drive me home and drink more whisky while she tried to get the money out of Arch. When I was fourteen she said she'd taught me all she knew, God help us, and anyway, now that the school was down to four kids they were putting her out to pasture and I had to go to the High in town. She died the next year."

"Too much whisky, I guess," said Beth.

"I reckon," said Bruno. "It's the whisky keeps us poor, me'n Arch. I know that."

"Why?"

"A bottle a week? Top shelf stuff. The first thing on the damn shopping list." He grinned. "Had to get special permission from the cop to buy it. Not twenty yet, see. Why am I telling you all this crap?"

"I dunno," said Beth. "I didn't ask."

"It's just that Arch gets to me at times. He's — he's . . ."

"Impossible?"

"And some. He's a bit mad, I know that. This place was a farm when he first bought it. Never ran much stock but it's big enough that it could've made us a good living. He's just let it go downhill. He can't do anything. Well, he never could. Couldn't even hammer in a nail. He used to manage a shop in town. When he was over fifty he cashed in his super and his savings, and he already had a bit of money from his own dad who'd died in England. Used the lot to buy this place and it's just gone backwards ever since. Funny old bugger. He's right; he couldn't harm a blowfly. When I got back here from Auckland, after being away, he had sheep that came inside, his four geese had become fifty and they all had names and lived in the garden. There were at least thirty cats, three magpies, and two stinking old billy goats living under a corner of the house."

"It sounds lovely," said Beth. "What did you do?"

"Do? Nothing very much. They were his." He gave a short laugh. "I did reduce populations a little bit when the opportunity arose but then after his accident I had to get really brutal. It's all well and good having a blind father but I didn't need a broken-legged one from tripping over half-wild cats and geese and goats. And it's all well and good Arch going on about the sanctity of life but it's that dead animal I brought in on the bike that's gonna help pay for this week's whisky. Arch never thinks of that."

"Yes," she said. "Well I've got to go. I really do. Stella says for you to come and have lunch with us on Sunday, and I think it'd be a good idea. We could have a look at that Shakespeare thing, or the poetry, after lunch."

"Yeah, okay," he said, "that'd be good. But I do need to take more than just a look at Shakespeare."

They stood and Beth moved to carry on down the road. Then she spotted them. "Look," she whispered, touching his arm. "Look." She pointed. Just ahead, the black nanny goat and white kid had come out and were browsing in the grass and weeds. Beth and Bruno stood still. "They're quite lovely . . . even if you say they are pests."

"Yeah," he raised his voice slightly and the goats took off.

"You didn't shoot them?"

"No," said Bruno.

"Why not?"

He looked at her. "Because you said you liked them, that's why." He turned back up the road.

Chapter 11

"Your mother's coming," said Stella quietly.

"No," said Beth. "No!"

"You've got to see her, honey."

"I don't! I won't," said Beth.

"She's coming on Sunday. For lunch."

"Oh, no. You said to ask Bruno, and I did."

"God, no. I'd forgotten. Better put him off, hon."

"No," Beth was grim.

"Be it on your own head, then," said Stella, shaking hers. "She's bringing what she calls her new boyfriend."

Beth walked out of the house, down the path and out the front gate. She headed away from the crossroads and into the gorge. She walked quickly, head down, with her arms folded in front of her, against that emptiness that drove in, flooded in on her. For days she had scarcely felt it. Now it was back in all its intensity.

She would not see her mother. She would not! If she never saw the woman again, it would be too soon. Never! Never! She went on walking. One foot after the other, without a thought as to what she was doing or where she was going.

Her mouth tasted sour and dry, and she swallowed against the dryness, involuntarily retching. She paused in her striding. It was coming on dark and a misty drizzle seeped over her, cold through the light sweater she was wearing. Her jeans were already soaked. But she felt nothing. She looked about her, registering some surprise at the distance she had covered. She was in the middle of the gorge. Little, almost no traffic. Leaning against the parapet of stone that edged the road she looked down into the turbulence of foaming, rushing water forcing itself through the rocks below. She kept looking and pulled herself up to perch crouched on the wide ledge of the stone wall, motionless, hugging her knees.

Beth didn't hear the vehicle and it wasn't until the Jeep was almost past the girl that the driver, concentrating in the half light, spotted the crouching figure. The Jeep stopped and reversed back to the narrow verge beside the stone wall. "Silly place to sit at this time of day," the woman driver called out. "Are you all right?"

Beth looked up. "I'm just sitting and looking."

"In this cold and wet? Ridiculous. Come on. Hop in and I'll take you home."

"I'm not going home. Not ever," said Beth, mistaking her meaning.

The woman smiled slightly, then noticed the girl's agitation. "Can't park here all day," she said matter-of-factly. "Beth, isn't it? Come on, get in. I'll take you up to the Lodge. It's just round the corner. You can dry out there. You certainly are soaked."

"It's okay," said Beth.

"It's not okay," said the woman more sharply. "It's almost dark. You're a hazard to what little traffic there is, and, I daresay, to yourself. Now, get in. Come *on*." An order.

Beth obeyed. "I don't know you . . ." she said, confused, "but you seem to know me."

"Ray. Ray Sullivan. Run the Lodge with my pal, Lesley."

Beth didn't respond. The drive, less than two minutes' worth, was enough for her to gather her wits. "Look," she said, as Ray parked the Jeep. "I'm very sorry, I lost track of time. Don't want to be a nuisance. I didn't know what I was doing."

"Oh, shut up," said Ray, in a friendly tone. "Come in and dry out and have a brandy or a coffee or something. I'll phone your aunt, then I'll take you home. No trouble. No guests in tonight, unless Les has lured some unwary traveller — and that'd be doubtful in this fog. Besides, we'd both like to meet you."

"Me?" said Beth, bewildered.

"Yes, you. Be good to meet someone we've heard so much about. Come on in."

They bullied Beth out of her clothes and into a hot shower, providing an outsized white towelling robe for her to put on while her clothes dried. Then Ray phoned Stella while Lesley gave Beth a bowl of very thick, hot soup. Neither pestered her with small talk. They sat in the large kitchen that opened onto an even larger living area of stone and plastered walls furnished with a scattering of sofas, easy chairs and floor cushions clustered about a raised island fireplace piled with logs. The women got about their business and left Beth to her thoughts. No prying, no questions. She was grateful.

"More soup?"

"It's beautiful — the soup, I mean. Well, I guess the whole place is." Beth tried to make conversation.

"Give us the bowl, I'll ladle some more in," Ray smiled. "Yes," she agreed, looking around, "it's not too bad. We're pleased with it."

"Do you get a lot of people staying?"

"It's coming," said Les. "Out of season at the moment, but when the fishing starts."

They talked of the fishing, and the building of the place, and Beth warmed to the two women as she started to warm again within herself. She didn't at first hear, nor register, the familiar put-put of Bruno's motorbike until it was too late and he was already inside the kitchen.

"Geez, you two! If you only knew the aggro this brute landed on me. Why can't you . . . Beth! What's wrong? Hey, what's up?" He looked around distractedly, dropped his plastic-wrapped load on the table and moved towards the young woman.

"Nothing. It's nothing," said Beth. "I just went for a walk and lost track of the time, that's all. Mrs Sullivan picked me up."

"Seemed to be the only way we'd get to meet the girl. After all," Les looked at Bruno, "we have heard quite a bit about her."

Bruno was unconvinced. "All the walking you do? You don't lose track of anything — are you sure you're okay?"

"Come on, Ray, we've got that tax return to do," said Les. "It's due by the end of the week and if we don't get it done we'll be well and truly up the creek."

"Eh?" Ray sounded puzzled, then caught the eye of her friend. "Be right with you. I'll just pour Rambo here a bowl of soup."

Then they were alone. She knew he was about to say something. "Don't — don't —" she put up a hand, "don't say anything. Please, Bruno. Don't say anything."

"Nothing I did?" he asked quickly. "Or said?"

"No, you fool. What have you done?" She looked straight into his eyes and the concern and care that she read there was all it took. She broke. Wave after wave of soundless, wracking, despairing sobs. He slipped from his perch on the table, took her in his arms and held her, stroking her hair. Stroking, stroking, until gradually the crying eased and she just slumped against him, exhausted.

Then she gathered herself and eased away from him. He didn't try to stop her. "Thanks," she whispered. "Thank you."

"Tell me about it?" he asked, very softly, as he reached out to touch the front of her hair.

She shook her head. "No," she sighed. "There's nothing."

"Tell me," he said again.

"Some day. One day I will." She touched his fingers and he took her hand.

"Have it your way," he smiled. "Just you remember that some day can be any day." He took out a particularly filthy handkerchief and dabbed at her face and wiped her eyes. "You staying here?"

Ray bustled loudly in. "Of course she's staying here. It's all jacked up with her aunt."

"No . . ." began Beth.

"Do as you're told, young woman."

"That's telling her, Ray," said Bruno. "She doesn't, though. You're charging her full rates, I hope? She is nearly seventeen and not a kid."

"Get away with you!" The woman laughed.

"Charge her double and then you can afford to pay me," said Bruno.

"I'll charge you with a pitchfork, you great brute. Make yourself useful and set that table. You can stay for dinner and there's a Thermos of soup you can take home for Arch — tell him there's no meat in it."

"I cannot tell my father a lie," said Bruno.

"Oh, ho, ho! Tell that to the birds. If that's the worst one you ever tell him he'd be lucky. And while I'm dishing up get along to that end bathroom and have a shower yourself. You look, and smell, in desperate need of one. You can hang that new towel rail in there at the same time. Screwdriver and drill are on the sideboard."

"I've been so worried, darling. Scarcely a word from you in all these long months. I was telling Gino on the way up . . ." The woman nodded and pointed. "You do like him, don't you, darling?" she whispered. "Gino, it's short for George. A real sweetie."

"I'm fine, Mum. Pretty busy. School's harder than I thought." Tense.

Stella's eyes darted between mother and daughter and then on to the man. Gino, bored, flicked through a stack of her sketches, trying hard to look as if he knew what he was doing. Fortyish, white shirt open almost to the waist against the cool of the day and in order to show off the last of a summer tan. Too many gold chains nestling among the greying hairs of his upper torso. Par for the course, Stella thought.

"I saw Susy and Jilly last week. They tell me school's a real hoot this year and they all miss you heaps and send lots of hugs, kisses and love," chattered her mother.

Susy? Jilly? Another world.

"Another drink, Gino?" asked Stella. "Lunch will be hours yet. I hope Prue warned you about my cooking. Sometimes it doesn't even happen. G and T again?"

"Ta," said Gino.

"Have you heard from Michael?" Beth asked her mother. "I haven't."

"He called last week. Collect, of course. They're in Brisbane. Well, he thought it was Brisbane. Construction site. Big money, or so he says, even if he did have to call collect. They're moving on to Sydney about June."

"That'll be nice," said Beth. Michael was her

brother. Six years the elder. Nothing in common. Never had been.

"Have you been to the doctor, darling?" Beth's mother didn't wait for a reply. "You said you'd take her, Stell."

"No need, Mum. I'm fine."

"Well, you're booked in for a final checkup with the specialist when you're home in May. Freshen my drink, too, Stell. Brrr," — she affected a shiver — "I'd forgotten how cold it gets out here. Gino, poppet, get me the cream and brown sweatshirt from the car, there's an angel."

"I'm not coming home in May, Mum. Cancel it. Don't need to see him. I'm staying here. I've got to work."

"You're coming home in May, Beth, and there's an end to it," said her mother. "Besides, it's Susy's big party. Seventeen. The big one-seven," she chuckled. "They'll all be there and they're all dying to see you."

"School's proving a bit of a struggle for her, Prue. Beth needs all the time —" Stella tried to inject a few words.

"Nonsense," said her sister. "School isn't the be-all and end-all of everything you wretched teachers make it out to be. Beth must simply start to pick up a few threads again at home. Besides, I need her help. I'm giving a couple of big parties for the firm — it's all wealthy Chinese from Hong Kong and Taiwan these days — and I can't be expected to do everything by myself." She sighed and looked out through the window. "Goodness, who's this coming up the path? Are you expecting a Maori visitor, Stella? Where's Gino? He simply doesn't like them at all. Bit of a racist, poor lamb, but rather sweet."

"He's coming to lunch, Mum. His name's Bruno. We're in school together and he's a friend."

Her mother's lips tightened. "You always did know how to pick them, didn't you?" Soft but sharp.

Stella shook her head, took a long drink and wondered why on earth Beth had persisted in this needless antagonism of her mother. She hoped it would not be Bruno who ended up as the meat in someone else's sandwich. She need not have worried.

"I lived up in Auckland for a couple of years, Mrs Paterson."

"How nice. Where abouts?"

"Don't think it'd be any part you'd be familiar with, Mrs Paterson. We used to hang round the city a lot. An awful lot," he smiled at her.

"It's about time they cleaned it up." Gino did not specify exactly what needed cleaning up, where, or by whom. "Take your life in your hands at nights. It's not safe."

"Yeah. Guess it can be a bit freaky," said Bruno. "It's all right when you know your way around, though."

"And you did?"

"Sh . . . sure. Sure did."

"Did you work?"

"Sometimes," said Bruno. "Depends what you call work."

Beth remembered a few of Brenda's words and played some more with her salad.

"Know what I'd like to do with most of 'em," said Gino. "City's not safe after dark. Street kids, glue sniffers and all the rest."

"String 'em up, eh?" said Bruno, looking at Beth.

"Cut off the bloody dole for starters. That's what I'd do. That'd show 'em."

"No use, sweets. They'd get it somewhere else," said Prue Paterson. "They'd take it from you and me, one way or the other. What d'you intend doing when you finish school, Bruno?"

"I've got to finish school first, Mrs Paterson," said Bruno. "And there's not much to do around here . . ." He gave a little giggle. "Might have to end up on the dole, eh? That's if you haven't cut it off by then." He looked at Gino.

"Cut it out, Bruno," said Stella. "You know quite well what you want to do."

"If I finish school, Mrs Paterson, I hope to go on to university and do a degree in social science. How would I ever use it? Dunno. Maybe end up working with some of those street kids you see around the city. At the moment I don't know, and getting through this year is all I've got time for at the moment."

"How interesting," said Prue Paterson.

Beth toyed with the same lettuce leaf as before and Gino helped himself to more lasagne. Stella poured herself another drink.

Prue bailed up her daughter in the bedroom. "The same rocky path, young woman?"

"Leave me alone, Mum," said Beth, not needing to ask what her mother had meant.

"What on earth do you think you're playing at? Haven't you learnt your lesson? Is this what I brought you up for? It strikes me you're your father's daughter all over."

"I can't help that," said Beth. "I'm tired, Mum. When are you going? Leave me alone."

"Oh, yes. The one mistake I ever made was leaving you alone. God knows I had little option. Had to earn a living, and you and your brother were never cheap. Fingers to the bone and sucked dry, and all for what? Dammit!" on a rising temper. "Why did I let you come here? Crackpot Stella and her crackpot bloody notions. You can pack your stuff this instant and come back to town with me."

"No."

"You'll do as you're told, madam. Is this all the thanks I get?"

"I'm not coming back to town, Mum."

"You are."

"I'm not and you can't make me. There's no way you can make me." They stared at each other, both breathing hard, their dislike of each other so intense it was almost tangible, almost like a third person in the room.

Stella came in. "Cut it out you two."

"Bug off, Stella," said her sister. "This is partly your fault and it's none of your business."

"I've sent your Gino for a walk," said Stella. "I think, from the look on his face, it might be the first step he's taken for years that was further than to the fridge or to climb into bed or to that vulgar little Jap thing he's driving with the winking eyelids," she prattled, trying to defuse the situation. She looked at her sister. "Nothing's my fault, honey, and you know it. And you, Beth?" She spread her hands. "Lord knows, kid, you're your own worst enemy. There's no point taking her home, Prue, if she doesn't want to go. Sure and certain recipe for further disaster."

"She can't stay here. I won't have it!"

"She can stay as long as she wants," said Stella.

"I won't pay another cent for her keep. I'll wipe my hands of her."

"God, Prue. Is that how you measure everything? Cents and dollars? I don't give a stuff if you pay or not. I like having Beth here."

"Honey, in her own way she loves you. She's not some two-horned devil or demon. She's your mother. You're just so alike. When I came into your room, plonk in the middle of your little spat, in spite of the fact she's carrying a few more years and a bit more weight, you even look alike."

"Don't you tell me I'm like her, Stella. Don't tell me that."

"Honey, you are. Both as stubborn as wretched mules."

"I don't even think about her, Stella."

"Ho, ho. You think about her all the time and work away at keeping that little pot of hatred simmering, blaming her, laying on her many many things that are — or were — your own fault. She's some sort of focus for everything you do. Think about it, Beth."

"I don't know what you mean," said Beth.

"You don't want to know what I mean, Beth," Stella said quietly.

Beth sighed. "I don't know."

They sat among the uncleared mess of lunch. Stella stoked the fire and tended her gin. "You're two sides of the same coin. You've never given her credit for anything and she's surely to goodness not all bad. It's often just the way she says things." Stella managed to smile.

"You're part right there, Stella. But it's not the *way* she says things. It's *what* she says."

"And you think life's been any bed of roses for her? Look, Mikey was eight and you were only two when your father took off. Left her with nothing. Think about that. No help from anyone and a load of debts as big as Everest. Well, she not only got that act together but managed to bring you two up at the same time. Poor old Prue." Stella bit at her bottom lip. "God, girl, don't you see what she does? Everything you hate her for is no more than some all-out try at protecting you, arming you against what happened to her. Did she ever tell you that she was only your age when our old man — old devil that he was — forced her up the aisle four months pregnant and into the arms of a man she should never have married. Yeah, she was just a kid herself."

"I did know," said Beth. "And I do give her credit for some things. It's just that all of what you say has turned her into something different and her values and stuff are . . . well . . ." She sighed. "Well, I just hope my values are never like her values, put it that way." All of a sudden she smiled. "I'll give Mum credit for one thing. Reckon there's no one else alive can sell real estate like her."

"Yes," said Stella thoughtfully. "And that in itself is a miracle. Prudence, at your age? Selling anything at all? Couldn't have sold a lifebelt to a drowning man. Couldn't even add up."

"It's not that, anyway, Stella. You know that. You know what it is I can't ever forget and I don't think I can ever forgive."

"Honey, come over here." She held out her arms. "I'll give you a hug, but it should be your mother holding you — if you'd only let her!" Stella held Beth closely. "I've got to say one thing more, honey. It's often what we do to ourselves that we can't forgive; far, far more than what others ever do to us."

Chapter 12

Bruno tried to study. He prepared a very early dinner for himself and Arch and then shut himself away. Set himself a good three chapters of 'read and digest'. No use. In one eye and out the other. So much for British colonial history. In one eye and out the other. Arch played a tape. Loudly at first, and then very loudly. One aria, over and over, until the song seemed to explode inside Bruno's head.

In one wild swipe of his table top, Bruno swept to the floor the flotsam and jetsam of British colonial history; notes, books, the lot. Paper flew. He stood up, prowled his small room, then rested his hands against a wall, palms forward, fingers spread, softly thumping his forehead against the wall in time to Arch's music. "Oh, God," he dragged out the profanity. "I'll never do it." He sat on the edge of his bed and reached for a cigarette.

Arch played the tape again.

"What does it matter if I never do it?" Bruno said to himself. "Like, who cares? Who gives a stuff? Can't do it, anyway. None of it. Doesn't go in. Doesn't stick. Doesn't do nothing, anything. Don't understand it. It's not even interesting. Boring, boring, boring, bloody boring!" he went on talking in a soft monotone. "Feeling sorry for yourself, eh boy? Like, why should anyone care? Self-pity. That's what it's called, eh boy? When the going gets rough, the tough get going. Eh? When the going gets tough? Rough? Stuff? No easier for Beth. Beth." He sighed, took the line of least resistance and lay back on his bed with his hands beneath his head, thinking about her. He wished she was right there on that bed beside him. Right there, and certainly not to have a chat about British colonial history!

What did he want with her, anyway? What did he really feel about her? Stupid questions. Friendship? Sure. Anything more? Stupid question. Of course he wanted more. Much, much, much more. Didn't he? God knew she was as screwed up as he was. Wasn't she?

And what did she want from him? Anything? Was it him or was it Arch who drew her up the road? Couldn't be Arch. Surely not. But whoever knows what draws anyone? In the end it was a toss-up which was the more confusing. Beth Paterson? Or British colonial history?

He decided it was time to take on Arch, Maria Callas and *Tosca*. He went through to the living room, turned down the volume and waited for the inevitable. It didn't come. It was almost as if the old man had been doing nothing more than using the music to attract his attention. "Is that you, Bruno?"

The absurdity of the question struck Bruno and was enough to wipe out a good three-quarters of his ill temper. "Who did you think it'd be, Arch? Want a cuppa?"

"Sit down, boy."

"You want a whisky?"

"Sit down. There's something I want to say to you."

"Please yourself."

"In the top drawer of the Welsh dresser, at the back, there are two letters. I want you to remember that when I'm gone."

"Where are you going, Arch?"

"Don't rile me, son. You know what I mean. Just listen," said his father.

Bruno looked at his father. He got up and poured Arch a whisky and put it in his hand. "Okay, Dad," said Bruno, responding to the seriousness in the old man's voice and using the term he hadn't used for years. "There's a drink. Go on. What d'you want to say?"

"Don't know when you're worse, lad," Arch smiled up at him. "When you take everything I say as some sort of joke or when you try to be serious. Anyway," — he took half the whisky in one gulp, paused briefly, then poured what was left down his throat — "I'm not going to last forever, boy. Today? Tomorrow? Next month or next year? Doesn't really matter. It's as well to be prepared."

Bruno smiled, and said nothing for a moment. If it was his death that the old man was talking about, it'd be the first thing he'd ever really prepared for during life. "I guess you're right, Arch," he said, as much to get his father going again as anything.

"There's a letter for you. Tells you what to do with me when I've gone."

"What to do with you, Arch?"

"Far as I'm concerned, boy, you could dig a hole for me in the garden. I've always fancied being planted under that scrubby little pin-oak over past the lilies. Might help it along a bit. However, the powers-that-be take a dim view of such proceedings, so don't try it. I'm plumping for the next best thing," said his father. "The other letter is for my solicitors. Post it."

"Reckon it's a good few years away yet, Arch. Another whisky?"

"Just put the bottle beside me, boy. Don't forget what I said. Where's that girl of yours? Hasn't been up to see me for a week or two."

"Beth?"

"You've got more than one? Nothing would surprise me," his father chuckled. "I don't think I ever talked to you about the birds and bees. Remind me to do it some time."

All of a sudden Bruno laughed. Loud and very long. Eventually his father joined in.

"God, old man! You've left it a bit late. I think I'd managed to work most of it out before I was seven. What with all the cats and that old white billy goat you used to have. And once Miss Forsythe used her pet guinea pigs to explain a few details. Said she'd be sacked if the Minister of Education ever found out but that didn't worry her because she'd taught him too!" He chuckled.

"Old Alma? Nearly forgotten her. Nuisance of a

woman," said Arch. "Had a booze problem, you know."

"Is that right?" said Bruno, looking at the whisky bottle.

"Fool of a woman. Wanted to marry me. Didn't know that, did you?"

"Why didn't you?" Bruno was curious.

"Once round the mulberry bush was enough for me. Besides, I didn't think she'd make a good mother," Arch announced.

"What? Were you thinking of having another family?" Bruno grinned.

"Stupid ass! I meant as a mother to you," said his father.

"That's unfair, Arch. Old Alma was more of a mother to me than my real one ever was. God, just mention her name and I can feel that supplejack: 'This is going to hurt you, Bruno, very much more than it's going to hurt me.' She was right, there. It did."

"Don't think ill of your own mother, son."

"I don't," said Bruno. "I don't think of her at all. There's nothing to think about."

"She did what she had to do," said his father, but did not explain further.

"What I've got to do is get back to British colonial history," said Bruno, standing. He looked down on his father. "I'll remember what you said, Dad."

"I know you will, son," Arch said, reaching out towards Bruno. "Give me your hand. Indeed, if you could spare a moment, just hold me for a while. Please." Quietly.

Kneeling, the young man took his father in his arms and did as he was asked. It had been a long time since they had held each other. Bruno was struck by his father's physical frailty. Just bones, really. Skin and bones kindled by some spark, some small flame that kept the whole alight — and that could reflect even from sightless eyes.

Paths did not cross. Bruno did not see Beth for some time. As autumn drifted into an early winter and No-name Road turned from goat track to waterfall, he assumed, when he had a moment for thought, that the hazards of the trek into the hills had put her off visiting.

He spent less time at school, reasoning that it was better to spend it at home where he found it easier to shut himself away to study. Times with Les and Ray at the Lodge became fewer. Once a week for odd jobs and a loan of the Jeep in order to get into town to shop for his father and himself. If it were fine he'd give them a weekend afternoon for anything else they needed done. Hunting was all but finished now. A few brace of wild duck was just about all. Instead of the game he normally supplied, he'd slaughter and dress a sheep for them from the small stock they kept in a paddock along the river bank. Fishing was in full swing, and the Lodge was often full. Bruno's Saturday afternoons frequently extended to dishwashing, serving, bottle-opening in the evenings and then a hurried dinner with Les and Ray and a scurried motorbiking back home round the gorge.

"I wish you'd stay, Bruno. The fogs are horrific now — dangerous. It's raining cats and dogs tonight," said Les.

"Or, if you let us help put in a phone for you, you'd be able to ring Arch on nights like this," said Ray.

"Have you any idea how much a phone connection costs these days when you live up a road with nobody else on it?" Bruno asked. "I checked it out soon after Arch's accident. It was hundreds back then. Probably thousands now. We ain't got that sort of money and neither have you. Besides, it's only twenty minutes on the bike."

"Take the Jeep tonight. Bring it back tomorrow and pick up your bike then," said Ray. "Do as you're told," she said firmly as she sensed a refusal coming.

"For a change," said Les.

"Okay," he smiled. "Mind you, in this weather, getting up No-name on the bike is easier than in the Jeep. Still, if I get stuck you can blame yourselves."

"And take that leftover strudel for Arch. It doesn't seem the Japanese are all that keen on it."

The rain had eased but the fog was still down by the middle of the next morning when, in first and second gears only, he eased the Jeep back down the greasy track. He reached the ford, going down, the same time as Beth reached it, coming up. "Get in," he called. "We'll come back on the bike. Easier by far than walking."

"True," said Beth, and climbed in. "Not that I was coming to see you, anyway. I was calling on Arch. I've made him another cake," she giggled.

"God help him," said Bruno. "Last one just about crucified his false teeth. Hope this one's better." He laughed.

"I'm not going to bite," she said.

"Yeah, that's right. That was the problem Arch found with your last cake. I think he said it was sort of like concrete."

"It was not!" she objected, laughing. "I may not be the world's best cake baker but I'm not all that bad, and I think I'm getting better. They do taste better than they look."

"Yep," said Bruno. "As I said to Arch, at long last he'd found the one advantage to being blind. What's it with you two, anyway?"

"What do you mean, and slow down."

"I can't," he said. "We're actually slipping across this bit but it's not a problem. We climb up the other side and that'll slow us down." He negotiated a no-road section of No-name Road. "I hope," he added.

She held on tight and answered his question. "He's the nicest old person I've ever met and I can talk to him . . . I'm even getting to like Maria Callas."

"She's dead, you know," said Bruno. "She died of a broken heart. So they say. I got this theory she actually died from the sound of her own voice."

"I wasn't asking you," said Beth. "And I now know the story of *La Traviata*."

"She died too."

"I know."

"They're always croaking in that stuff — the operas — that Arch likes. Either they're croaking or they're praying. Me? Well, I'm generally praying they'll croak!" They came out on the highway. Bruno allowed himself a sigh of relief.

"You didn't have to drive so fast just to impress me," she looked sideways at him. "You're as bad as Vic Witt." Another side glance.

"Okay. Quits. You leave my driving. I'll leave your cooking. Did he ever try anything else with you?"

"Funny, I think his one experience might have been enough," said Beth. "Brenda tells me he's turned over a new leaf, changed all his spots and anything else you can think of. She's thinking of going out with him."

"Yeah," said Bruno. "Two of a kind, if you ask me. Thick as bricks, too."

"That's unfair, Bruno. And it's not true. Let's face it, kid, they're both doing better than you and me."

"Kid, yourself. And we're gettin' there, kid. We're gettin' there. Don't ask me where. Anyway," he turned into the Lodge driveway, "we're here now, and don't let Les and Ray talk you into staying for lunch. I've gotta get back and do some work. Besides, we can have a go at eating your cake when we get back home," he grinned.

They stayed for lunch.

"Should get you to hose the Jeep down before you go," said Les to Bruno as he and Beth made moves to leave. "Did he ever tell you how we first met him, Beth?"

"No," said Beth.

"It's time we weren't here," said Bruno, walking towards the door.

"Five minutes won't hurt," said Les.

"Takes you five hours to tell this story," said Bruno. "Besides, it's Arch. He thought I'd be straight back." He was smiling. "He'll be so worried."

"Go on, tell me," said Beth. "How did you meet him?"

"That fog's coming down again," said Bruno. "Better be on our way."

"Well, it was after he got back here from his time up in Auckland," said Ray.

"Boring, boring. She doesn't want to hear this crap," said Bruno.

"She does," said Beth.

"Only job he could get round here was as the Stop–Go man on the roadworks."

Bruno sat down again. "Just remember," he said to Beth, "they really love telling this one. They even practise it on the Japanese who come and stay and who can't speak English. Every time they tell it, they add little bits. By now it's three-quarters lies."

"Good," said Beth. "Go on, please."

"The worst Stop–Go man God ever created," said Les.

"Being a Stop–Go man is just about as boring as telling stories about it," said Bruno. "Like, what's to do except flick that stuffing sign round; stop, go, stop, go."

"Most Stop–Go men get it right. It's not too hard," said Les.

"Should be Stop-Go person. Not man," said Bruno. "I thought you were a feminist."

"You were a Stop-Go man, mate," said Ray. "Make no mistake about it. Don't try and dilute your responsibility. No Stop-Go woman or Stop-Go person could ever be as bad as you were."

"See what I mean?" said Bruno to Beth. "It goes on for hours."

"Yeah. It's good," said Beth.

"Gets better," grinned Les.

"To cut a long story short . . ." said Ray.

"Thank you God," Bruno looked upwards.

". . . on the day in question, twirling his sign like some demented drum major or cheerleader twirls a baton, and with his little walkman radio thing tucked in his little pocket and headphones suffocating his little un-shelllike ears, he stuffed it up good and proper," said Ray. "Along we drive on our lawful business, Les and me. 'Go' says the idiot with the sign. And what happens . . ?

"Ray, Les and the Jeep end up slap-bang in an ocean of steaming asphalt almost up to the hubcaps, with a truck bearing down on us smothering the whole lot in chip metal, gravel, and about to smother us similarly . . ."

Les took over the telling. "Ray jumps out to try to stop the truck, which doesn't seem to have seen us, and ends up ankle deep in the black sea. Les tries to reverse — there's hot tar everywhere — I think hell must be something like this! The nice white Jeep is now piebald and what does the Stop-Go man do?"

"Don't know," said Beth, choking with laughter.

"He just stands there and he says, 'Oh, sorry lady. I think I got it wrong, eh?' "

They were all laughing now.

"It's years ago," said Bruno. "I was just a kid then. Child labour, really. Read all about that in British colonial history."

"Well the child labourer got sacked on the spot," said Les, "And a good thing, too. I felt like hanging him, lynching him, drowning him in his own tar."

"Yep, I should've taken it to the Labour Court," said Bruno. "Unfair dismissal, or something. Would've won, I bet. Big damages, I reckon."

"Yes, there were," said Ray. "Cost the road people an arm and a leg before it was all over."

"I'm surprised you're such good friends," said Beth.

"It's her fault," said Les, pointing to Ray. "When we were finally helped from the mess, cleaned up just a little bit and had got on our very sticky way, who should we come across, shuffling down the road, still wearing his headphones, but looking a little worse for wear and very sorry for himself, but this lunk."

"Hunk", said Bruno, "that's the word you're looking for. Hunk is the word." He pointed at Beth. "She told me."

"Lunk," repeated Les. "And what did Ray say?"

"Go on," said Beth. "And lunk is definitely the word you need."

"Ray said, 'I feel a bit sorry for the kid. Let's give him a lift.' I won't tell you what I said or where I said I'd lift him. After all, I am a lady," said Les. "However,

I generally do as I'm told. Story of my life, that one. We stopped and we gave him a lift." She paused, smiled, and looked at the others. "Well, I must've, eh? Otherwise it's unlikely we'd all be sitting here today."

Chapter 13

"Nick Jenkins is having another party. Next Saturday. Nick's olds are off to a wedding or a funeral or something, and everything's all ours. You gotta come," said Brenda. "Won't take no for an answer."

"No thanks, Brenda — the cup of coffee, I mean. I'm trying to give it up. I think your coffee is a health hazard. In fact, I know it is!"

"Don't change the subject, woman."

Beth sighed. "It's—it's very kind, but ..."

"But nothing. Come? Please? Please, please, please?"

"Why are you so keen to get me there?"

Brenda looked at her. "There's something bugging you. There has been all year, and I'm not going to pry ..."

Beth stopped a smile. "Of course not."

"Well, I'm not," said Brenda. "Still, if there's ever anything you feel you'd ever like to tell me ..." Eagerly.

"There isn't," Beth looked at the other girl. "All right, then. I'll come."

"Great!"

"I'll bring Bruno."

"What?" A small shriek. "No! Who?"

"Bruno. Bruno Petrie."

"I thought that's who you said. No. That won't do at all. Besides, I said I'd . . . er, get —"

"Me to come by myself? Brenda Macaulay, you're as muddy as the coffee you make. No. You want me? You've got to invite Bruno, too."

"It's not my party," said Brenda.

"You seem to be in charge of the invites," said Beth, reasonably. "One word from you and I bet this guy Jenkins'd invite King Kong."

"He might invite King Kong, but he wouldn't invite Bruno Petrie," Brenda sat down. "You're not — you know — well, seriously seeing him, are you?"

"I'm usually quite serious when I see him," said Beth. "There's not much of a giggle to be got out of physics, King Lear and British colonial history."

"I mean, like, going out with him?"

"Well, I went for a ride with him in his friends' Jeep just last week. Is that going out?"

"Those two old ducks who built that lodge? They're loopier than Stella. Sorry, dear. But it is the truth. Look, Bruno just wouldn't fit in. He's too old!"

Beth laughed. "Come off it, Brenda. He's only about two years older than us. Must be about the same age as that Jenkins guy."

"Have you managed to have a good look at what's going on? What's growing out on their farm? Have you? Latest I heard, it's at least a thousand plants. Maybe even more. And it's all growing where the cop spotter chopper hasn't got a hope of seeing it. You must've seen something."

Beth laughed. "There's nothing there, Brenda. Nothing. God, if he was into it like you reckon, he wouldn't be riding that clapped-out motorbike. Or bothering to come to school, come to that."

"Laugh your head off, woman. Laugh! Go on, laugh. It's all part of it, I've told you that. It's an elaborate cover, that's what my cousin's mate says. The motorbike, the mad old dad, they're all part of it."

"Brenda, I don't know much about growing anything, but I'd say that in early winter round here nothing'd have a snowball's chance of growing."

"What about his pack of killer dogs, then? You must've seen them. Everyone knows he's got them."

Beth sighed again. "He's got one old pig-dog called Primrose. That's it. He's just a pet, really."

"There's a whole pack," said Brenda. "Vic told me."

"Vic Witt? I don't know how he'd know."

"Petrie set them on him one day," said Brenda.

"I think I know the day you mean," said Beth. "Are you sure?"

"Sure am sure. Vic and his mates — Craig and Andy, they're nice guys and you'd like them — went out for a hunt, and it wasn't even on old Petrie's land. They got a bit separated and quite by accident poor Vic ended up on the wrong side of a fence. Anyone can do that out hunting, Vic says. Next thing he knew, he was surrounded by this pack of killer dogs and Bruno Petrie jumped out of this bush waving an AK forty-something — that's a big gun — wilder than hell and yelling, 'Hey, you boy! You get off my bloody

114

land eh!' and set the killer dogs on Vic. It's the truth. Now, why would he do that if he had nothing to hide?" she said smugly. "You tell me that. Anyway, that's what he did and Vic says him and Craig and Andy are going to bide their time and wait till Petrie's away somewhere and then they're going to go and get all the plants."

"They'd have to wait till the killer dogs were away, too," said Beth.

"Hmm. Wonder if they've thought of that? Probably not. Better warn them. They're not too bright, none of them."

"I've got to go," said Beth.

"Party! Saturday. Don't you forget," said Brenda.

As winter drew its first claws, Beth settled into a routine. The work at school became no easier but the time she spent on it meant she was coming to grips with at least the core of her course. Most weeks she'd have at least one session with Bruno, generally lasting a couple of hours, either up at his house or at Stella's. They would doggedly go over and over and over one or two aspects that puzzled or confused them.

"This way, some of it's got to stick," she said to him, gritting her teeth.

"Not necessarily," Bruno smiled. "But I reckon bits of it are. Sure is easier with two of us. I know it's helped in English." He looked across at her as they sat in the clutter of Stella's living room. "Any idea yet what you're doing next year?" He tossed aside study notes on *King Lear*.

"Not really. So much depends on this year, doesn't it?"

"What d'you want to do?" he asked.

"I doubt if I'd get in but what I'd really like to do is a degree in engineering," said Beth. "Maths is my strongest subject and, at a pinch, physics is okay. If only I hadn't had that time out last year."

"Didn't know you had," he said.

"Well, it wasn't . . . well, not very long," she said hurriedly. "Can I make you a coffee?"

"How long?" he persisted.

"I'm going to have a cup. Wonder what's keeping Stella?" She changed tack again. "Engineering school's sure hard to get into."

He gave up. "Well, judging by the way you fixed up my bike, and keep on fixing it up . . ."

She laughed loudly. "I don't think the engineering I want to do has very much in common with fixing motorbikes!"

"I know that," Bruno said. "I was just thinking of it as a sort of indication of the sort of thing you're good at. You think I'm one big thicko, don't you?"

"Sure do," said Beth. "Sure do." A car horn tooted in the driveway. "There's Stella. I'll put the kettle on."

It wasn't Stella. It was Brenda. "Tried to phone, but our line's down . . . nah, that's a lie. Mum's letting me use her car so I'm just cruising round everywhere. I told her I was desperately worried about old Lear, and that's the truth, and had to talk it over with someone. I can always get her car when I show just how academic I am, bless her. Old Lear is certainly a bit of a worry."

"You've come to the right place. Come on in. Exactly what we are doing."

"We? Didn't know Stella was into Lear," said Brenda as she shrugged off her jacket. "Oh!" she said, as she walked through to the living room. "I thought it was Stella."

"Stella's at a PTA meeting," said Beth.

"Does she go as your parent or as a teacher?" asked Brenda. "Hi, Bruno."

"Hello, Brenda."

Beth made coffee for the three of them while the other two sat in silence. "We could read bits of Act Three together," Beth called out. "That might help a bit." Continued silence. "Then refer back to the notes?"

"Yes," said Brenda.

"Okay," said Bruno.

Beth carried the mugs in and they sat, sipping silently. "Unless you two've got a better idea," said Beth.

"A better idea would be for me to give up school," said Brenda. "I'm sick of it, anyway. What the hell am I going to do with any of this?"

"Be a bit of a waste," said Bruno. "You're doing quite well."

Brenda looked surprised. "Would never have thought you'd notice," she said. "You duck in and duck out, put your head down, do your stuff and push off."

"Of course I notice," he said.

Brenda looked at him. "I just don't know how you have the time for school as well as running that big farm of yours," she said, taking a meaningful look at Beth and then tossing aside her copy of *King Lear*. "It sure beats me how you do it."

Beth tried to change the subject. "Is that Stella's car? You'll have to move yours, Brenda."

"Won't be Stella. She'll be hours. They're having wine and cheese tonight, Mum told me," said Brenda.

"We don't run it as a farm any more. Just hills, bush and scrub," said Bruno.

"No farming at all?" Brenda was not giving up.

"I'd like to take a look at Act Two, Scene Two," said Beth.

"My father let it all revert," said Bruno.

"How is your father?" asked Brenda. "Haven't seen him for years. Used to see him all the time outside the — the . . . er . . ."

"Pub," finished Bruno. "He's all right, thanks."

"I'm so glad," said Brenda. "What about hunting?"

"Well, he never did any," said Bruno.

"No, no; I meant, what about hunting on your farm?"

"Well, there's not much," said Bruno. "What do you want to go out after?"

"It says on page seventeen of the study guide . . ."

"Have you got guns up at your place?" asked Brenda, picking up her coffee mug. As she sipped she kept her eyes on Bruno.

"Yep," he said.

"What's an AK forty-something?"

"Yeah. That's a gun, all right," said Bruno.

"You got one?"

"Hell, no." He laughed. "First, I could never afford one. Second, well, it'd be a bit more than I needed for a few goats and things."

"Just wondered," said Brenda.

"I've got a twenty-two and an old shotgun," said Bruno.

"A sawn-off one?" Brenda looked eager again.

"Well, now you come to mention it . . ." Bruno laughed. "Look, I thought we were going to look at Lear." He looked at Beth.

"Do you like gardening?" asked Brenda.

"More coffee, Brenda?" asked Beth.

"No," said Bruno. "Do you? Like gardening, I mean."

"I've never tried it," said Brenda.

"Neither have I," said Bruno. "Don't know one end of a plant from the other."

"The end with the leaves or the flowers or fruit is the part that sticks out of the ground," said Beth. "It's not hard."

"It must be very boring for you, Bruno, on that farm of yours after living up in Auckland and everything you did there," said Brenda.

Beth had taken enough. "Look, lady! Let's get on with this damn play."

"Well, all right," said Brenda. "I was just making conversation over coffee. Don't get your knickers knotted. You take things far too seriously, Beth. That's what I'm always telling you." She looked at Beth and winked. "Now, Bruno, there's a big party out at Jenkins's on Boundary Road on Saturday and if you'd like to come, well, I know Beth is."

"Beth isn't," said Beth. "Or, least she hasn't made up her mind yet."

"Can't," said Bruno. "I'm working."

"Doing what?" asked Brenda.

"Dishes. Down at the Lodge. They're full and I work there Saturdays."

"What a pity," said Brenda. "Now let's get on with this stuffing play. After all, that's what we're here for, isn't it?"

Chapter 14

"What's the hurry?" asked Ray.

"No hurry," said Bruno, unloading the dishwasher.

"Tell that to the marines. What's in the bag you dumped at the door?"

"Nothing," said Bruno.

"Going somewhere?" Ray smiled at him. "Come on, man, I know the signs."

Les came through the swing door with an armful of dishes. "Bruno! Coffee! Where is it?"

"Still filtering," said Bruno.

"Well, it'll have to do. They're getting a bit bolshie out there and it's time I poured some coffee into them." She returned to the dining room.

"Leave the coffee," said Ray. "I'll do it. Leave the damn dishes. We're nearly finished, anyway. Go and see your lady."

"Hey . . ."

"Don't hey at me, young man," she smiled.

"Okay," said Bruno. "We're going to a party."

"It's a bit late," Ray looked up at the clock. "You should've said."

"Coffee!" Lesley roared back in through the door.

"Coming," said Ray. "Bruno's going."

"Busiest night we've had for months and you're letting the help go early?" Les raised her eyebrows, questioning.

"He's taking Beth to a party."

"Why didn't you say," said Les. "Oh, to hell with them," she nodded towards the dining room. "I'm taking five." She cleared a corner of a table and perched. "Where's the party?"

"Out on Boundary Road."

"Take the Jeep," said Ray.

"The bike's okay." Bruno reloaded the dishwasher.

"The Jeep!" insisted Les. "And that's an order. Bring it back tomorrow and bring Beth for lunch. Come to think of it, bring her aunt, too. We'd like to get to know her. And this lot leave in the morning, for which we should all be truly grateful."

"The bike's all right," repeated Bruno.

"Of course it is, for *you*, my fine-feathered friend. Certainly not with Beth on the back. And not at night. Do as you're told. Now go and change. Use our shower."

He did as he was told.

The two women looked at each other when, a few minutes later, he wandered back in and rummaged around looking for the keys to the Jeep. "Good heavens! It's the male equivalent of Cinderella. Where on earth did you get that jacket?" Les shook her head.

"Got it cheap off a mate up in Auckland when I was there," said Bruno. "Never worn it. It was always too big till now. Does it look all right? I think it's a good one."

"I can tell it's a good one," said Les. "How cheap? No. Don't tell me. I don't want to know. It's certainly not too big now. Beautiful leather."

The black jacket was of a loose, blouson style, beautifully cut. He wore it over a plain white T-shirt with a pair of tight, faded blue Levis.

"Fine-feathered friend, indeed," said Ray. "Now, get going. The keys are in the Jeep, exactly where you always leave them."

"We won't be late, Miss Gordon," said Bruno.

"I don't care how late you are, Bruno. I'll be asleep, anyway. I'm just so pleased she's finally going out somewhere other than for a walk." Stella smiled at Bruno. "And I think you can drop the Miss Gordon bit. I know damn well you call me Stella — and a lot of other things — behind my back," she chuckled.

"Okay, Stella." He grinned back.

"Do we have to go?" asked Beth.

"No," said Bruno.

"Yes," said Stella. "And a good pair of peacocks you make, the two of you. Go and strut your stuff. Haven't seen that outfit before, hon. Suits you. When you've finished with it, you can give it to me. I'm not too proud to accept hand-me-downs from a child." She looked appreciatively at the soft grey and red sweater, the grey matching the trousers Beth wore.

"We'll be back in half an hour," said Beth, winking at Bruno.

"Go on. Get out, both of you. I want a lovely quiet Saturday night, all alone, watching whatever pap's on the telly, and then a nice mug of cocoa. That sure is a mark of my increasing years. Go!"

"Sounds great, Stella," said Bruno. "Can I stay?"

"Get out!"

As they left the house a fine rain was falling and they ran to the Jeep. "Look," said Bruno, as they settled themselves into the vehicle, "we don't have to go. We could go somewhere else."

"Like where?" asked Beth. "The old quarry?" She laughed. "Look, we will go for half an hour. Brenda would never forgive me if I didn't turn up at all and I have got quite fond of her. She's worked on this one for weeks. Besides, I want to see her face when I turn up with you."

"She did invite me," said Bruno.

"Yeah. I know she did. Still, I don't think you were expected to accept. And you did tell her you were working."

"It's not even her party," said Bruno.

"Every party round here — and it doesn't matter where it's held — is Brenda's party. It's her job, her function in life," said Beth.

"Some job," Bruno snorted. He looked at her as he started up the Jeep. "You sure look good," he said, shyly. "You smell good, too."

"Come on," she said, very quickly. "Let's get it over with, and — and . . . thanks."

"What for?"

"Nothing. Come on."

The only difference, Beth reflected, between this party and the summer poolside party was that the party-goers were wearing more clothes and it was held inside rather than out. The noise was the same, the crowd was the same, the music didn't appear to have changed, and the sticky orange liquid seemed to be pouring out of the same jug with just as great a frequency. The Jenkins' spa pool was already serving the selfsame function as had the Macaulay's swimming pool.

"You came! You came, you came, you came . . ." shrieked Brenda. "And who's this you've brought with you? Amazing!"

"You know damn well who it is, Brenda," Bruno scowled.

As luck would have it, at the moment of her greeting the music stopped, the noise of laughter and conversation ebbed and the arrival of Beth and Bruno became, for a moment, a focus. Brenda worked at filling the gap. "Hey, look guys! Look what the cat's dragged in. It's Paterson and Petrie."

There were one or two nods from those Beth knew, a smile here and there, but, in the main, it was all eyes. Half showed surprise and the other half hostility.

It was only seconds. Someone had the sense to change the tape and Bruno said, "Where can we get a drink, Brenda? Not gonna touch that stuff you're carrying. Looks like poison."

"It is. I tried it once," said Beth.

"Come on in," said Brenda. "Drinks are in the kitchen, Bruno, and the kitchen's through there." She pointed. "Get one for yourself and one for Beth. Off you go." She turned to Beth as Bruno pushed through to the kitchen. "Told you so," she whispered. "Now you can see. They hate him. Or else they're scared of him, and I think I am too. Mind you, he sure looks something, doesn't he? Never seen him look that good before. Now it'll be even worse. Every guy here'll be jealous of him, too, and you don't look too bad yourself, kid," she prattled on.

"They don't know him, Brenda," said Beth. "That's all it is."

"That's not all it is," said Brenda. "And here he is," she raised her voice.

Bruno was fully aware of the reaction his being at the party caused. He was partly puzzled, partly amused by it all. "Not a bad party, Brenda. Thought there'd be more here, though." He decided to bull his way through the whole thing, for Beth's sake rather than his own. He looked at her as she sat, eyes down, playing with her glass.

"Just the usual gang, Bruno," said Brenda. "Don't think you two know Nick Jenkins," — she grabbed at a passing arm — "it's his party."

"No, I don't," said Beth. "Hi."

"Yeah. I know Nick," said Bruno, grinning. "Nick and me started at High together, way back. G'day mate." He stood, half a head taller than the other, and put out his hand.

Nick took his hand, a little reluctantly, and muttered a greeting.

"Good party," said Bruno to Nick.

"Yeah. Not bad. Glad you could come. Brenda said you might." Nick looked at Brenda. "They're yelling for food out in the kitchen and I don't want them wrecking the joint. You know my Mum. Can you give us a hand, Brenda?"

"Sure," said Brenda. "See you two later."

Beth and Bruno were left alone. Left well alone. "Reckon we can go yet?" Beth asked.

"Nope," said Bruno.

"It's—it's terrible."

"You're the one said we should come."

"I was wrong," she said.

"Yep."

"And you're no help."

"Nope."

"And, if you say that again . . ." She looked up.

"We gotta have two more drinks, two dances and at least a bite of whatever they're cooking up in the kitchen. Then we can go. And you gotta smile. See!" He grinned very broadly.

"Where did you learn all this?" asked Beth. "You sound worse than my mother."

"Oh, I picked up one or two things since me'n Nick started at school together. See, there are rules for these games. Every game has got rules."

"This is a game?" she asked.

"Sure is," he answered.

"I wouldn't've thought you cared," she said.

"I don't. Not for me," said Bruno. "But I do for you. You're at school with this lot more than I am."

"You win," said Beth. "Let's have the first of our

two more drinks and then we'll have a dance. That's if you really want to. And—and ... sorry."

"What for?"

"Getting you to come here."

"Least of my worries," said Bruno.

In the end they stayed longer and, while the frost didn't completely thaw, a few of the others there joined them for a chat, Brenda doing her hostess-best and Bruno and Beth doing all they could to show just how much they were enjoying themselves.

"Do you want to come in?" Beth asked Bruno when they arrived back at her aunt's house. "Coffee?"

"Better not," he said. "It's late. Stella will be in bed and the road'll be helluva slippery in this rain. Easier on the bike than in this," he said, tapping the steering wheel. "Yeah, why not? Just a quick cup." He smiled.

He stood in the kitchen, his back against the sink bench, while she made them a drink. "Enjoy yourself?" she asked, with a wry smile.

"About as much as you did,' he said.

"That little! Gee!" She looked at him. "Why don't they like you?" she asked, bluntly. "It's almost—almost as if some of them are scared of you."

"Don't know," he said. "Don't care either. Probably it's just the outsider thing. I've never been part of them. I never knew them; they never knew me. It doesn't matter."

"I think it does," said Beth.

"Really it doesn't," he insisted. "I was pretty tough,

pretty bad, when I first came into town for school at thirteen or fourteen. Most of this lot wouldn't know that, because they're younger, but they have heard stories, and stories always get blown up. You know that. Thanks." He took the coffee mug from her. "I guess I was a bit violent. Mind you, it was a case of I was and I wasn't. It was more that I didn't know what to do, didn't know how to behave. Not ever." He pulled a face. "Old Arch and Miss Forsythe might have given me a good start in some things, but when it came to knowing how to behave, well, that sure wasn't one of them."

They continued to stand in the kitchen, speaking softly. "You do know that they tell the most horrible, god-awful things about what you got up to in Auckland."

"No, I didn't know," he looked at her slyly. "How could I?"

"I don't believe them, though," said Beth.

"Why not?" He smiled. "They might be true. What sort of things?"

"No. No. I'm not ... nothing, really."

"Go on. What sort of things? You can't say something like that then not tell me. Besides," he gave a soft chuckle, "I'm curious to know how bad I was. How bad I am!"

She felt stupid and wished she had said nothing. "Well," she began, and swallowed, "they say you lived rough, sort of street-kid type junk, and that you got into crime, thieving and all that. Pretty tough. Pretty rough."

"Yeah," agreed Bruno, "it was."

She gulped. "It's true?"

"Yep. That surprised you, didn't it?"

"Mugging?"

"Yep. Sure. Cars, too. It's all true. They got it right." He gave a slight grin. "Wonder where they found out from?" he said, a puzzled look on his face.

"I—I don't know," she said, very quickly.

The grin turned into a laugh. "Hey, it's over. Done with. It's all in the past. Don't worry, I'm not going to waste them, as us hoods and crims say, for talking about it."

"Not—not drugs?"

"Nope on dope, kid. Oh," — he spread his hands — "tiny, tiny wee spot of dope, weed. Nothing at all really. Not interested." He glanced at her again. "Tried glue once. Got stuck to the plastic bag." He looked at her out of the corner of his eye.

"You're laughing at me, aren't you?"

"Yep," he said. "Sure am. So what? So I lived rough for a while. What the hell? Hundreds do. Didn't do me too much harm. You may not want to believe me but I met some great kids. I made the first real friends I ever had. Friends like I never ever had round here."

"But . . ." she started.

"No, let me finish. You asked. I was looking for something. I think I told you that once before. I thought I knew what I was looking for. Now . . . well, I'm not so sure. I guess I was looking for some sort of roots. I found a lot of things but I didn't find those. Took me a couple of years — and that's not long, not really — to sort of find out I was looking in the wrong place," Bruno talked on, his voice quiet. "It's true. I did find them. I found them right back here — back where I started. Back here" — he jerked his head towards the window — "up that bloody awful track with old Arch and his, ours, my useless land" — she took his mug and made him another cup of coffee — "and it took me a helluva lot of thinking and working out and I don't suppose I've done it all yet ... and why do you want to know all this? Like, all I want is to know about you and you never say anything."

"Yeah," said Beth. "One day, yes, one day ..."

"I'll hold you to that, lady," said Bruno. "Now, just one thing then I gotta go. I never ever mugged any little old ladies and I didn't murder my best mate by throwing him off a motorway overbridge." He winked at her.

"You knew all the time what they say about you, didn't you? You ... words fail me!" Beth grinned at him.

"Of course," he said. "What d'you think I am? Thick?" He put down his mug, took hers from her hand, held her arms lightly with his hands and kissed her softly on the lips. "Goodnight," he said. "And thank you. Don't forget we're going out to lunch tomorrow." Then he was gone.

Chapter 15

Beth answered the telephone. "No. No, he's not here yet ... Yes, it is a bit late." She bit her lower lip. "What time did he say we'd be there?" She paused. "Yeah, that's when he said he'd be here." Another pause. "No. No, she wasn't coming anyway. She's up in Auckland for the day. It's an art exhibition and she's got something in it. Bruno said he'd tell you. Look, I'm sure he'll be here any minute, Les ... okay ... okay. See you soon." She replaced the receiver and wandered to the front door.

The day was clear and very cold. Beth shivered slightly as she walked down the path to the front gate. Nothing in sight. She walked back inside. The first gnawings of concern started to bite. Although often pressed for time, Bruno was seldom late. She paced the living room, idly stooping now and then to pick up a book, discarded magazine or a coffee mug left lying about. Ten minutes. Quarter of an hour. She picked up the telephone.

"Ray? It's Beth. I'm going to wander up No-name. He certainly should be here ... We were a bit late last night and he could have slept in ... or a puncture, something like that." A tight little laugh. "Mmm, yes. I'll murder him for you as well ... okay, bye."

She grabbed a parka from the hall stand and left the house. Her feeling of unease grew and she started to jog up the lower sections of the road until she reached the ford. No mud puddle now, the water was shallow but fast and she hopped from boulder to boulder, praying she didn't slip. Then she slowed, peering down into each damp, dank, scrub-covered gully. Common sense told her this was not really necessary, the mud of the roadway showed only one set of tyre tracks, and they went straight ahead up the road. As yet there had been no return trip. For all that, she went on scanning the roadside, remembering what had happened to his father.

The half-walk, half-jog took forty minutes. She was breathing hard into the cold air as she crested the last rise leading up to the gravel and grass plateau where the Petrie house stood. The Jeep was there, parked by the back porch. A sigh of relief.

Beth knocked on the closed door. Nothing. She knocked again. "Arch! Bruno!" she called. "It's me, Beth." She waited. Nothing. "To hell with it," she muttered and opened the door. "Bruno?" She peered in. Still no response.

Then she heard the sound. It came from the big room, the living room. "Bruno? Is that you?" She took two or three paces into the kitchen. The sound, a wail, was louder. A thin, keening wail. Like an animal sound. It came from the main room. Her concern coupled with fright but she moved on in, one hand to her mouth, biting a knuckle. "Are you there, Bruno?"

The body of Arch Petrie was on the floor. Beside him, half crouched, half prone, one arm protectively across his father's body, was Bruno, still dressed in his clothes of the night before.

"Bruno!" Beth moved quickly. "God! Bruno," she crouched, "What—what . . .? Arch . . ."

The thin, high pitched wailing didn't stop and it took Beth a few seconds to recognise it came from Bruno. "Bruno!" she was half yelling. "For God's sake, Bruno . . . Arch . . .?"

Bruno turned and stared at her and Beth knew in an instant that nothing she could do or say would likely penetrate his consciousness. His face was streaked, filthy, the dust of the floor and the rug on which Arch's body lay had mixed, encrusted with tears and mucous. Bruno's eyes were vacant, opening and closing in a glazed non-comprehension, not focusing on her and only barely aware of the presence of anyone else. She moved to touch him and a low growl from a corner of the room made her start. It was Bruno's dog.

"It's okay dog. It's okay Primrose. It's me." She spoke softly while extending a hand to touch Bruno's shoulder and arm. He flinched slightly at the touch. She felt the tremble, and at the same time, the rigidity in him. She stood silent for a moment or two, thinking, then bent down again. "Bruno," she spoke clearly, "I'm—I'm going to get someone. Get some help. You stay here," she said, unnecessarily.

Beth walked from the house and stood in the back porch. She realised she was trembling. Realised, too, that she was crying. She breathed deeply once, twice, wiped a hand across her face and set out. She took a few steps, looked at the Jeep and then back at the house. She bit her lip, then made up her mind and walked to the vehicle and got in. The keys were in the ignition and it started with no trouble.

She slowly circled the plateau then headed off down the road, changing gear only from first to second as the truck slithered and slipped into the perilous mud of the roadway. "Do it in low. Don't brake. Do it in low," she repeated over and over to herself, wondering, as she slowly slid side on into a corner, if it may not have been quicker to run.

At last she reached the ford, negotiated the stepping boulders and eased the Jeep down the lower stretches to the highway. She did not stop at Stella's, drove through the gorge much too fast, and turned into the gateway of the Lodge.

"Lord, Bruno! It was lunch, not dinner. Where've you been!" Ray called from the doorway, then, "Beth! Beth, what's wrong?"

"Arch is dead," said Beth.

"Dear God, no."

"He's up there with him, Bruno is. I can't get him to move," Beth started to cry. "I think he's half dead himself."

It took time and much effort to get Bruno away from the side of his dead father. It took the combined efforts of Beth, Les and Ray, the valley's one policeman, the doctor and the local undertaker.

"I'll give him a shot," said the doctor. "You won't notice much difference. He's exhausted now and he's in a shock. It'll help him relax a bit and maybe sleep a while. The body's got to be taken. Post mortem and all that. Bert?" The doctor looked at the policeman.

"No sweat," said the cop. "We'll get the boy and the women back down and then worry about the rest."

"The boy and his dog," said Les, looking at Primrose whining softly at Bruno's feet. Oblivious to the activity around him, Bruno sat slumped in a chair, not taking his gaze from the bedspread-covered body of his father. He bit absentmindedly at the nail of one thumb. Eventually, as the effects of the sedation seemed to relax him slightly, Les and Ray took him by the arms, half lifting him to his feet and easing him from the room. Seeming to realise what was happening and what was required of him, Bruno offered no resistance. Instead, he shrugged off their hold on him and stood for a moment in the doorway, weaving slightly, then supporting himself. His mouth worked and then, absolutely silently, he cried; tears welling, falling down his face. Slowly he moved back into the room and knelt by his father's body. Gently he pulled back the bedspread. The others looked on, silent.

"I love you, old man. I loved you and I never told you I loved you. Never told you . . . never . . ."

Bruno stood. He walked to the dresser and opened the top drawer. He rummaged around for a moment and then took out two envelopes. He looked towards the others. "Come on then," he said. "If I gotta go, let's go," and he left the house.

Dear Son

When you read this I'll be dead. I can't think that you would have bothered to steam it open prior to my demise.

There is little to say of my life other than I did what I chose to do and have few regrets.

I leave you little other than this parcel of largely useless land which I love. I leave you content in the knowledge that you love it as much as I do. Do with it as you will.

The sole regret I have in departing this world is that I must leave behind the one great joy and singular achievement of my life: you. I love you. That is all there is to be said.

Shed no tears for me. I am egoist enough to know that you will remember me. As I am, so are you. In part at least.

Should you choose a sentimental path of remembrance you may care to occasionally play an operatic aria or two on that infernal machine. Who knows? You may even come to enjoy and appreciate what you hear.

To the final dread details. Have me cremated and use my ashes to fertilise a very small portion of those acres I have happily neglected. A few blades of grass may be in for an unaccustomed and pleasant surprise! No clap-trap parson or preacher is to prose over my bones. You are now a man and old enough to do what I want done. Over my boxed remains kindly read verses 1-8 of Chapter 3 of the Book of Ecclesiastes, beginning, 'To everything there is a season, and a time to every purpose under heaven.' Use my old King James Bible and none of this modern nonsense. You may care to add a brief personal comment, not that there is likely to be anyone there other than you and maybe the undertaker, and I don't like the idea of you talking to yourself. I certainly shan't be listening. From thence to the funeral pyre. You may also care to play a track of the incomparable Maria singing "Pace Pace Mio Dio' from The Forces of Destiny. Peace peace, my God! I doubt the existence of such an entity but a little insurance doesn't hurt.

Finally, while there isn't any fortune, you will find sufficient funds with my lawyers to pay for the barbaric ritual of my funeral, a bottle of good whisky for yourself for afterwards and a small nest egg for your future.

Remember, dear son, to the best of my knowledge we travel this way but once. Make the most of the journey! Arch.

Three days later Bruno Petrie followed his father's wishes. In the event, Arch Petrie had nine mourners, not counting the undertaker. Lesley and Ray, who travelled the hour's drive to the nearest crematorium with Bruno. Beth, with Stella and Brenda Macaulay who had insisted on coming. Bert Cooper, the local cop who drove over for the ceremony with the longtime publican and his wife from the Criterion.

"Arch Petrie was my father." Bruno stood next to the coffin. "He left me instructions to say a few words, read a bit from the Bible and play a piece from an opera that he loved. It won't take long, none of it. Afterwards Ray and Les say we're to all go back to the Lodge and drink a bottle of whisky. That's what my Dad wanted us to do.

"He lived for quite a long time, did Arch. Even so, it's not easy for me to say goodbye to him. He was a funny old guy. He did no harm to nobody and he lived his life as he wanted to live it." Bruno's voice trembled but he controlled himself. "I will miss him," — he paused — "I guess I'll miss him for the rest of my life."

Beth Paterson sat very still, head bent and hands clasped tight in her lap. She made every effort to keep her mind, her thinking, on the words and the sounds she was hearing and to block out any thought, any memory of that last small funeral she had been to.

"I don't mind admitting I'm a bit disappointed," said Brenda to Beth and Stella on the drive back. "Like, it's the first funeral I've been to. Sure didn't take long."

"Thank God," said Stella Gordon. "It's the best one I've ever been to. Least we didn't have to listen to a load of lies."

Beth stared out of the car window and said nothing. She thought of Arch. She thought of Bruno. She saw the old man, the pale, sightless eyes a-sparkle as he listened to his incessant music. Saw him as he gamely munched into the cakes she had kept on baking. Heard him, heard the irony, as he tackled poor Bruno on yet another score. Heard, too, the affection and the love that underscored whatever sin of his son he was pointing out.

"And where, I wonder, were all of Bruno's friends and great mates from Auckland? I was dying to see them," said Brenda. "You'd think they'd have all turned up. They stick together at times like this. I've seen it on the telly."

Beth thought of Bruno. Of the twice she had been round to the Lodge in the days between Arch's death and his funeral. "I don't know what to say," she had said to him.

"Nothing much to be said," he had replied, and had turned away from her.

"Do you think Bruno will stay on at school?" Brenda leaned over from the back seat and spoke louder to Beth.

"Dunno," said Beth. "Ask him."

"I thought he would've told you," said Brenda.

"No. He hasn't said. He hasn't told me anything," said Beth.

"Oh? I am surprised," said Brenda. "And I do hope there's more than a bottle of whisky for us to drink back at the Lodge."

"It's not a party, Brenda," said Beth.

"It is, sort of, honey," said Stella. "I could surely do with a good whisky at this very moment. I don't know. As I get older winter seems to come sooner and colder than it ever did before. Funerals come more often, too." She fiddled with the controls of the car heater.

Chapter 16

Bruno Petrie cleared up his father's few things, tidying away rather than disposing of. He straightened the house, gave up school, and shut himself away.

Les drove him through to see his father's lawyer. "No great problem," he was told. "Legal ins and outs take a little while but we'll pay for the funeral in the meantime. Any other bills?"

"No," said Bruno.

"You've enough to manage on? Your father's pension will have been stopped by the welfare people."

"I earn enough for me," said Bruno. "Arch's pension only ever kept him. Well, almost."

"There is money," said the lawyer, handing Bruno a sheet of paper and pointing to the bottom line. "It'll come to you in, oh, two or three months. We can let you have some in the meantime should you need it."

"It's okay," said Bruno. He gave a slight, wry smile. "Pity the old sod didn't let me have it before."

"Oh?" the lawyer raised his eyebrows.

"Yeah. There's enough there for the phone we always needed and for a car or a truck. Now it's too late to help him."

The lawyer understood. "I think that what is there

was intended to help you and not him," he said gently.

He didn't hear the knock on the door and Beth was in the living room doorway before he was aware of her presence. "Hi," she said. "I brought you a cake." She nodded at the plastic bag she carried. "It's in here."

"Hi."

She moved to the stereo and lowered the volume on Maria Callas. "How about making us a cup of tea? Use the silver teapot, I like it," she said cheerfully. "Come on." She moved through to the kitchen. "It's very tidy," she commented, looking around.

"Would you like it?" Bruno asked.

"Like what?"

"The teapot. You can have it if you like. Sort of in memory of him," said Bruno.

Beth looked at Bruno. She spoke softly. "Yes and no," she said.

"What do you mean, yes and no? Either you'd like it or you wouldn't." He sat down at the kitchen table and lit a cigarette.

"Yes, I would like it, but I don't need it to remember Arch. Like, well, I'd only known him for a few months but I know I'll never forget him. Never. Yes, I'd like it, but I'm going to leave it here. It can be mine but it belongs here."

"That's stupid," said Bruno.

"No it's not. I know what I mean." Beth looked at him. She took over making the tea and unwrapped her cake. "It's a currant cake. Never tried one before."

"Looks like you put sheep dags in it." He smiled for the first time. "They sure look black and they sure look hard."

"Arch would've liked it," she said.

"Yeah. Until your back was turned," said Bruno. "Then you should've heard what he said about your cakes."

"I've photocopied all my notes from school for you. When're you coming back?"

"I'm not."

"What?"

"You heard me. Like," and he shook his head, "who wants that crap, anyway?"

"You do," said Beth. "You do. You know you do. God, Bruno! What're you going to do? Sit up here forever? It's three, four weeks. We've had the holidays. I've been home and come back — I've even half, well, quarter patched up things with my mother. Now it's school again. What are you going to do?"

"Dunno," he shrugged.

Beth poured the tea, cut two large slabs of the cake and pushed the plate towards him. Bruno picked up a slice and began picking out the currants and eating them. He put down the cake and pushed the plate from him. "I'm not hungry."

"What's wrong?" she asked.

He stood up and looked across at her. "What's wrong?" he sneered. "What's bloody wrong? You know what's wrong. My father's dead! That's what's wrong. My father's dead!" He was yelling at her.

"I know. He was an old man, Bruno. I think, as

much as anyone is, he was ready to die." She reached out towards the angry young man and touched his arm. He pulled angrily from her.

"What would you know about it? What would you know about it, eh? All your fancy clothes and that junk . . . your posh snob mother and all that, and school with other snob kids and snob houses and everything . . . just everything. What would you know about it?"

"Shut up!" She yelled now. "Shut up!"

"What would you know about anyone dying who you'd loved? Nothing! That's what. Sweet nothing!"

Beth sat silently for a moment. Then: "My baby died," she said, very quietly.

"You don't know nothing." He hadn't listened.

"My baby died."

"Your what?" He half heard.

"He was four days old and he died, and I loved him," said Beth. "That's what I know." Her face was a mask. No sign of emotion. Her jaw was clenched. "My baby died and my mother said it was all for the best and there was no one else, no one else at all who ever really cared. Only me."

Bruno looked at her. He was breathing hard. "Yeah. Well. That's bad. But, so? You lost a kid who'd hardly ever lived. There's a bit of a difference, isn't there, between a father you've known all your life and a baby that lives for a couple of days? Isn't there?"

The mask of her face cracked and contorted. She looked at him for a handful of seconds and, gripping the table edge, she hissed "You bastard!"

Turning, she ran from his house.

Chapter 17

Bruno sat and stared at where she had been. His mouth had gone dry and he licked his lips and swallowed. "Oh, God," he whispered. "Oh, God, what have I done?" He stood up. "Beth! Beth!" He ran to the back door and stared into the hazy silver light of the late afternoon. "Beth!" he called again.

There was neither sign nor sound of her. He ran across the clearing and peered down the road. Nothing. "Beth!" he yelled more loudly as he started to run faster, slipping and sliding in patches of frost that had not lifted from the night before, that made perilous the shaded parts of the road. "Beth, Beth, Beth!" He was screaming her name.

Running now as fast as he was able on the frozen ground he both saw her and had gone past her before he was able to stop. Turning too quickly he slipped and fell heavily on his side, his ankle twisted beneath him. Pain shot from foot to knee but it didn't stop him standing and he hobbled, breathless, to where she stood. She stared at him as she leaned, slumped against a tree.

Bruno put one arm out to support himself against

the trunk of the tree and he drew Beth towards him and held her with the other. He looked straight down into her eyes. "I never meant that. Oh, God, I never meant that," he said. "Beth, you gotta believe me. Please. I never meant what I said."

They stood, clinging tightly to each other. She began to cry and he did too. No words for some long time. Finally each lessened their grip on the other and Bruno's hand shot out again to support himself against the tree. "You gotta believe me," he said, very quietly.

"I better get you home," said Beth. "Lean on me."

"Reckon we better lean on each other," said Bruno. "What d'you reckon?"

She did not mistake his meaning. "Reckon you could be right," she said. "We'll see. Come on."

They made slow progress back to the house. "It's a fracture," she said with certainty. "I'll bind it up for now, but it'll hurt."

"It's hurting now," he said.

"It's going to hurt more yet," she said, a measure of pleasure sounding in her voice.

"You're a sadist," he said.

"You're right," said Beth.

He hopped to a living room chair and flopped. "Get me a cigarette, please?" he pleaded.

"No," she said, tearing a towel into strips of cloth. "I mean, you've already wrecked your ankle, how about giving your lungs a break?"

"You *are* a sadist."

"I'll bring the bike round," said Beth. "You can go on the back. I think I can get us down to Stella's without breaking any other bits of you — or of me!"

"No," he said.

"No what?"

"I don't give a stuff about my ankle," said Bruno. "Another hour or more won't kill me. I'm going nowhere."

"You're doing as you're told," said Beth.

"God, Beth! You sure sound like your mother."

"I'm her daughter," said Beth.

"I'll do whatever you say," he said seriously, "but you give me an hour first, and—and make me a cup of tea with a bit of your cake." He gave a small, shy grin. "Mind you, thinking of that, I'm even surer that you're a sadist."

"All right," she said. "Be it on your own head. Or ankle."

Beth made tea, sliced cake and brought a tray through to where he was resting. She threw his cigarettes and lighter across to him. "At least Arch didn't smoke," she said.

"Look where it got him," said Bruno. He looked across at her. "Tell me about it," he said. "Tell me everything you could've told me a long time ago."

She knew what he meant. She shrugged slightly. "It's as I always said, there isn't very much to tell."

"You also said that one day you would tell. This is the day," said Bruno.

"I guess it is," said Beth. "I had a baby last year."

"I always thought it was something like that," said Bruno.

"I don't know why."

"Actually, I thought you might have had an abortion," he said.

"I wouldn't have one," Beth looked at him.

"Who was the father?"

"Someone. No one. It doesn't really matter."

"Might have mattered to him."

"I think it did," Beth said. "Least it did a little bit. He was my age and he was quite nice. It was a party. That was nice, too," she smiled a very small, crooked smile. "Was after a sports meeting. Athletics. Never knew I was a runner, did you?"

"I knew you were a walker."

"The guy, Grant, was from another school. Well, he'd have to be because St Mary's is only girls. I didn't even know him. Bad, eh?" she pursed her lips. "My first time, and I think his, too. It was—was . . . it was a nice party. Was at his place and there weren't very many there. One thing led to another, then to another and so on. That's it."

"That's the beginning," said Bruno.

"We did see each other a couple of times more, later on," she shrugged again. "But there was nothing there. Nice guy, but I wasn't really all that keen on him."

"You didn't know you were pregnant?"

"Of course I did. Eventually. Mind you, it took a while. See, I never did have very heavy periods. They were always next-to-nothing. Might've been because of all my running, fitness and that. Dunno. By the time I knew for certain, I was three months gone. By the time I told Mum I was halfway through and still not showing. I told you there wasn't much to tell."

"Bet the old manure hit the fan and the ceiling, then."

"Sure did." Beth looked grim. "Like, I was the biggest disgrace to hit our family for centuries even though . . . So, I said no way would I have an abortion, said I'd have the baby and it could be adopted out." She walked over to one of the three long windows and stared out. "Sometimes, just sometimes, I pretend that's what happened and it — he — is adopted." She turned back towards him. "Grant and his mother and father were in on it all. Wasn't very nice. He wasn't all that interested but he tried to be. I left school in the sixth month. St Mary's, being St Mary's told Mum not to send me back."

"What about Stella?"

"Oh, she didn't know about it. Not back then. Big family secret. Last couple of months I got put into a home for young mothers. Finished sixth form by correspondence. Didn't do a thing but I'd already done enough to get me through. The baby was born . . ." Beth sat down opposite Bruno and looked at him. "I can feel every minute of it, right now, right through me . . . I can." She paused for a while, looked down. Then looked up again. "The baby was born and I called him John."

"Come and sit by me," said Bruno.

"I'm not going to cry," said Beth. "Don't worry."

"I don't care if you cry."

"My mother came and saw him once. Grant did, too," Beth spoke very softly. "He was all right for the first three days and on that third day I made up my mind he was not going to be adopted and I'd tell Mum that. I didn't care what she said, I was going to keep my baby. He was just so—so lovely. Just so lovely. Oh, he was. I can see him now . . ."

"Come and sit here."

"I can just see him," she said and breathed deeply. "On the fourth day something went wrong. Respiratory, they said. That's his breathing. They tried everything, I think. Nothing they could do. He — he just died. In my arms." She stood up, looked at Bruno and said, very brightly, "Then there was sweet bloody nothing. Not a thing except for the ache and the pain and the emptiness and I thought it'd never go. Never, ever go. And I came up here to live. Like, God, how could I live with my mother who thought it'd all been for the best? How could I do that, eh? How? She meant it, too. She meant it, all right. You want to know something?"

"What?" he said.

She scowled at him. "You say you want the truth . . . well, there was nothing for me, nothing at all, until I met you. So there!"

"Come here." An order.

Beth held back. "And I didn't really know that until, well, just before when I ran out of this house and I thought . . . I don't know what I thought."

Bruno struggled to his feet and hopped towards her, almost cornering her. "You thought I'd let you down, that's what. I did, too. I let you down. I won't again. Not ever."

"Sit down," she said. "You look stupid hopping after

me like a mad magpie. Go on. Sit down. Yes, I think that's what I thought. And I guess that's what you did do." She sat down beside him and smoothed his hair, touched his face. "I might not forget what you said, but I will forgive you. You loved dear old Arch."

"He wasn't very dear most of the time," said Bruno.

"You loved him, Bruno. And you're grieving for him. Maybe all I was going to say back then was that first, you're not the only one who's ever grieved, and second, that the only thing that really does help is time. I know everybody always says that, but it's true. I think it has helped me. I think it will help you. It's just that it sure takes a lot of days, one after the other, after the other and on and on."

"I know," he said. "I think I know."

"I don't think you do. Not yet," said Beth. "But I am right."

"Yep."

"Now, Petrie, somehow I've got to get you down that hill. Come on."

"Nope."

"Not again," she sighed. "What on earth is it this time? Come on."

"Pain's gone, anyway," he grinned.

"Then let me kick it for you," she said, grinning back at him. "Just as a gentle reminder."

They looked at each other for a few moments and then Bruno took Beth in his arms and they kissed for a long, long time. "It seems like I've waited for that forever," he said, and kissed her again. "There's going to be a lot more of this."

"I hope so," said Beth, and kissed him. "I do hope so. I'm glad you waited though."

"Worth waiting for," he said. "I knew that eventually you'd be unable to resist me."

Beth kicked Bruno's ankle.

Chapter 18

At the beginning of October, Beth and Bruno gave a party to celebrate his twentieth birthday. "It'll be the strangest party I've ever had anything to do with," said Beth. "A bit of a weird assortment. It'll never work."

"Of course it will," said Bruno.

"The only good thing is they've all got to be down the road before dark or they're likely to go over the side and never be seen again."

"We could hire a tow-truck," said Bruno. "And an ambulance."

"And can you imagine my mother having a chat with Vic Witt?" she asked.

"No. But I can't imagine *me* having a chat with Vic Witt either," he said.

"It's Brenda's fault," said Beth. "I don't know what she sees in him."

"Didn't you go out with him once?" asked Bruno sweetly.

"Look, you . . . I'll make the cakes for your party, and it'll serve you right," she laughed.

"Yes, well, we'd better hire the ambulance in that case."

"I was perfectly prepared and perfectly able to do some of the food," said Beth.

"But wasn't it nice of Les and Ray to offer to do the whole lot?"

"I just wonder about that. Like, you know that saying? Did they fall or were they pushed?" She winked at him.

"Simply marvellous," breathed Prue Paterson. "And you own the lot, Bruno?"

"Most of what you can see, Mrs Paterson," he said.

"Call me Prue," said Mrs Paterson. "I'm not all that ancient. Gino! Come and look at this view!" She turned back to Bruno. "I've got this sweetest couple from Hong Kong dying to get their hands on something unique and rural. Promise you'll let me know if it's ever on the market. Gino!" and she moved on out to further admire the view.

Brenda and Vic arrived. "Well, Bruno Petrie, I'll say one thing for your road. It sure keeps Vic's hands on the steering wheel. Now, Beth. I'll take over the drinks for you. I just know you'll be quite hopeless at it and Vic's car seemed to develop a very nasty knock in it coming up that last mountain, so could you have a look at it for him? So, that's your mother, Beth? Cor! If I look as good as that at her age ... you do realise, Beth, that you look much older than your mother?"

"It's clambering under cars and poking in motorbike engines that's done it, Brenda. That, and your coffee in the common room."

154

"Happy, happy birthday, Bruno." Brenda stood on tip-toe and planted a kiss on his face. She giggled. "I almost forgot why we were here. What can you get for the man who's got everything, I asked myself? So, big bad Bruno, I'm still thinking about it. Ah, here's Vic now. He's too shy to ask you Bruno, but he wants to know if he and his very good mates Craig and Andy — they're nice guys even if they are a bit dumb — can come and do a bit of hunting up here and have a good old look around."

"Of course you can, Vic," said Bruno. "Anytime. Why haven't you said before?"

"I think it'll be your muffler, Vic," said Beth. "I can see it dangling from here."

"Eh?" said Vic. "Oh . . . er, thanks, Bruno."

"The clunking under your car, Vic," said Beth. "It's the boulders on this road. We'll grab a bit of fencing wire and tie it up before you go."

"Must have a chat to your Mum," said Brenda to Beth, "and find out all about you. I wonder where she gets her hair done? I'll be up in Auckland next month. Come on, Vic."

"So much for doing the drinks. Whose idea was this?" Beth asked Bruno.

"Hey, it's good! I'm enjoying myself," said Bruno.

"Food's ready," Les came in from the kitchen. "It's all out on the table. Everyone can help themselves. Call them, Bruno. Beth, dear, pour me'n Ray a drink. Nice and strong. One for Stella, too. Must get that dessert recipe from her. Looks a dream."

They ate. They sang 'Happy Birthday', and Stella

carried in the cake. "Isn't it superb," she called. "Beth made it all by herself. You won the battle this time, hon! God save my kitchen!"

"Beth made it? Beth made a cake?" Prue Paterson looked at her daughter. "Beth can't boil an egg."

"But she sure can make cakes, Mrs Paterson," said Bruno, giving Beth a hug and a kiss. "This one must just about be the greatest cake I've ever seen."

"Do you think blindness runs in the family?" Les whispered to Ray.

"No, but I've heard love's blind," Ray whispered back. "It must be. Still, it did save us having to do it."

"Let's wash it down with another drink. That might help." Brenda got busy. "We must have a toast, anyway. Give us a hand, Vic. Oops! Did you break the knife blade, Bruno?"

They all laughed.

When everyone had gone, Beth stayed behind and helped Bruno clean up and clear away. "I'd better go," she said, when they had finished. "You can run me back down in that wonderful new mean machine of yours." She nodded out the window.

"It's great, eh?" Bruno looked out at the small, red, near-new truck parked by the back porch. "Thanks for everything," he added, turning back to her.

"I should think so," said Beth. "Oh, yes, I gave Primrose his bit of cake."

"Is he okay?"

She laughed. "Why is it . . .?" she began.

"Do you have to go?"

"Yes," she said. "Stella'd be worried. But you can

make me a cup of tea in my teapot first, if you like."

He looked at her and smiled. "I don't want you to go."

"I don't want to go," she smiled back at him. "After all, this is just about our very last chance to come to grips with King Lear. Where are your study notes?"

"To hell with Shakespeare. I wasn't thinking of Shakespeare," he said.

"I know you weren't," said Beth. "Nor was I."

"Well?"

"I don't have to go for a little while, Bruno," said Beth.